MELONHEAD

MELONHEAD

Michael de Guzman

Farrar, Straus and Giroux
New York

Library of Congress Cataloging-in-Publication Data
De Guzman, Michael.
    Melonhead / Michael de Guzman.— 1st ed.
        p.   cm.
    Summary: Tired of living with his non-caring divorced parents,
Sidney, a twelve-year-old boy with an unusually large head, takes a bus
trip across the United States which becomes a journey of self-discovery.
    ISBN 0-374-34944-4
    [1. Voyages and travels—Fiction.   2. Identity—Fiction.
3. Runaways—Fiction.   4. Divorce—Fiction.]   I. Title.

PZ7.D3655 Me 2002
[Fic]—dc21

                                                    2002020863

To Marilyn

MELONHEAD

Prologue

The first thing Sidney T. Mellon, Junior, noticed when he walked into the large room with all the leather furniture and the polished wood smell was the big brown mole next to the judge's nose. There was a hair growing out of it.

"Sit down, young man," the judge said in a voice that measured each word as though it were an ounce of gold. "You take that one." He pointed to one of the two huge armchairs in front of his massive desk.

Sidney did as he was told, then watched the judge, who was pinch-faced and looked like a turtle, lower himself into the other chair, pull it closer, and smile.

Sidney smiled back. The judge's expression became serious. Sidney's smile faded.

"How are you today, Sidney?" the judge asked.

"I'm fine, thank you," Sidney responded, his voice taking on the tone and cadence of the judge's. "How are you today?"

"I'm fine, too," the judge said. "Do you know why you're here?"

Sidney turned to look at his mother, an intense, pretty, dark-haired woman with a slightly dazed expression. He looked to the other side of the room, at his father, who was blond, blue-eyed, lean, and fastidious of dress. Sidney didn't come close to resembling either one of them. With his short-cropped red hair atop his alarmingly large head and almost perfectly round face, he didn't come remotely close to resembling anybody he'd ever seen. Both his parents were smiling. They both had their lawyers with them.

"I asked you here because your feelings are important," the judge continued. "Do you understand that your mother and father are divorced and that they're not going to live together anymore?"

Sidney nodded. His mother and father hadn't lived together since last year. Before that they'd screamed at each other a lot, and a lot of it was about him, or so he thought, and he'd heard all of it. Then his father had moved out. No one had bothered to tell him why, and he was afraid to ask because he truly believed that it was his fault.

"Do you understand that your mother and father both want to take care of you and that we're here to decide where you'll live?"

He looked at his mother's hopeful smile and teary eyes, then at his father's kidlike grin.

"Would you like to live with just one of them, Sidney, or do you like sharing your time with both of them the way you do now?" The judge's expression was tinged with sympathy. He thought the size of the boy's head most unfortunate.

It took Sidney only a moment to process the question and its implications. He was being asked to choose between his parents or go on the way he was, split in half. But how could he choose between them? He couldn't bear the thought of hurting either of them, and surely that was what he'd do if he chose one over the other. His stomach erupted as hot juices of anxiety and panic swept through his small body. His chest pounded with terror. The drawbridge went up. The watertight doors slammed shut. He fixed his stare on the judge's mole, knowing that the judge saw him doing it. He didn't care. There wasn't anyplace else he could look. Then he saw the mole coming closer and closer as the judge leaned in toward him. Man, that was a long hair coming out of that mole.

"You look like a smart young fellow," the judge

said in a whisper that smelled of dust. "Plenty of brains in there, I'll bet."

Sidney pulled back with a jerk. More than anything in the world he hated it when people made reference to his head. He just hated it.

"So, which one will it be, your mother or your father? What do you want, Sidney?"

What Sidney wanted was to reach out and grab hold of that hair coming out of that mole and pull on it as hard as he could.

He was six years old.

1

The Fat of the Land

"Hey, Melonhead!" It was his stepbrother, William Devers, calling him. "Mom wants you in the house for dinner right now, Melonhead."

Sidney was sitting on a branch of the gnarled old fig tree, which was his secret place, hidden from view. He peered carefully from behind the trunk and saw his stepbrother searching for him from the back porch, his mouth slackly open, wonder permanently stamped into his otherwise vacant expression. Sidney had been in the midst of contemplating the fate of mankind, a regular pastime. What with all the bombs and biological weapons and the way people treated each other, such matters were much on his mind.

Overpopulation was his main topic of interest on this pleasant evening in August in Seattle, Washington. He thought it more than a little likely that one day soon there would be too many people on the pint-size planet that supported them all and, as a consequence, it would weigh too much and go flying out of orbit. Earth would shoot into space like a balloon losing its air in a hot rush. *Swoooooosh!* They'd all be gone. He showed no sign of hearing his stepbrother's grating voice. He never showed his stepbrother anything. William was two years older and a foot taller, and he'd called Sidney Melonhead from the moment they'd first met.

"William Devers," Sidney's mother, Meredith, had said on that occasion, "this is your new stepbrother, Sidney Mellon."

What chance did he stand with an introduction like that? Born with the head and the name to go with it. There was no escape. A nasty cosmic joke and he was the punch line.

Why his mother ever married William's father, Richard Devers, Sidney would never understand. He certainly wasn't consulted. She didn't even tell him about it beforehand. He was with his father in Los Angeles when it happened. When he returned to Seattle to spend his apportioned time with his mother, there stood his new stepfather. Before that moment he didn't know the man existed.

"Mom wants you now, Melonhead! Mom means it."

That was another thing. He hated it when William called his mother "Mom." She wasn't his mother. She was Sidney's mother. He didn't call William's father "Dad." He'd die first.

"Mom says to wash your face and hands, Melonhead! Mom says if you don't hurry she's going to get mad."

Sidney speculated about what his life might be like if William were strapped to a rocket and shot into orbit like a communications satellite, where he would spin around in the sky for seven years, then crash back to Earth, a fireball that exploded as it landed in the Pacific Ocean, then sank to the bottom. Sidney didn't like to think bad thoughts about people, but sometimes he couldn't help himself. He was at his best in a positive environment, one that was calm and without conflict. But that world didn't exist. Not when he had to spend equal time with both parents, which was what the judge had decided when Sidney wouldn't make a decision. He grinned. The rocket idea wasn't half bad. After his stepbrother went inside, Sidney climbed down from his tree. Then he went inside because he knew he had to.

At the table he took his napkin from its ring, which he'd made at the day camp he went to with his stepbrother whenever he was in Seattle in the summer. No one asked him. He was just sent. He turned his attention to the kitchen, waiting for his mother to appear. William was telling his father about his latest athletic triumph. William was a swimmer, a canoeist, a water-skier, a baseball player, and an all-around popular camper. Sidney was, at twelve, still short and pencil thin, and his head was still round and much too large for his body. His otherwise pleasant visage carried a hopeful expression and was naturally flushed. His red hair stood straight up in a long crew cut. The full effect of all this was that his head did indeed look very much like a melon. A cantaloupe was what usually came to mind.

He tried to focus on what his stepfather and stepbrother were saying. He could hear their voices, but it was like listening to music without words. And, anyway, he wasn't really there. That was another problem. He was almost never where he was. He spent very little time in the here and now. He daydreamed. His mind wandered. He usually didn't know what he was going to say until he heard himself say it, which was often the cause of great difficulty. He could defend almost nothing he did because he had no idea why he'd done it.

"Sidney!"

He realized that his stepfather had been calling his name and was waiting for a response.

"Sidney!"

"What?" he said too loudly.

"I'm talking to you," Devers said, giving Sidney the beady eye.

"I'm busy," Sidney heard himself say. I'm in for it now, he thought.

"Busy?" Devers could barely believe he was being challenged.

"I'm thinking," Sidney said. "My brain is presently occupied."

"You're a rude boy, Sidney. You have no manners. How many times have I told you to pay attention at the dinner table? You could take lessons from your brother."

"He's not my brother," Sidney said. Too late to take it back.

William smiled and held up his hands like he was holding a big ball and mouthed, "Melonhead."

"You're the only one in this family who doesn't try to get along," Devers said, his voice on the verge of being nasty. "I've tried. Your brother has tried. Your mother has tried."

"Tried what?" Meredith asked as she carried a platter of pork chops into the room.

"All of us have done our best to get along with your son, who doesn't seem to be the least bit interested in getting along with the rest of us," Devers said. "It's a personal insult."

Her face clouded over with unhappiness. It was an old story. "Sidney means to get along, don't you, dear?" She gave her son that look, the one that pleaded with him to cooperate with whatever was going on. "You do try, don't you?"

Sidney felt himself being sucked into the middle of something he wanted no part of. It was like being hooked to a tractor beam and pulled into the Death Star. He looked at his mother and nodded his head, then stared at his plate. Somebody please save me, he thought.

"It just takes Sidney a little longer," his mother said.

"He hasn't made an inch of progress in three years," Devers retorted. "He doesn't put himself out for anybody. He's selfish and secretive. He refuses to participate. He won't accept help."

"That's not altogether true," his mother said.

"And all you do is defend him." Devers's voice cut through the quickly gathering tension. "He's going to have a sorry life if somebody doesn't straighten him out." Devers served the pork chops, placing the one with the most fat on Sidney's plate. The potatoes and vegetables were passed. Everybody bowed their heads to say grace. Sidney flicked an angry glance at Devers, who caught him doing it.

"Bless this food which we are about to receive,"

Devers said, eyeing Sidney harshly, "and make us ever mindful of the needs of others. Amen."

Sidney looked around the table as the others dug in; then, as inconspicuously as he could, he cut the fat off his pork chop and pushed it over behind his potatoes.

"Don't hide it, boy, eat it," Devers said. "A growing boy needs some fat in his diet."

"Not really," his mother said. "Not too much of it, anyway."

"Eat everything, waste nothing," Devers said. "It's all food."

"I won't," Sidney heard himself say. "I won't eat fat."

His stepfather was on him so suddenly he had no time to move. He heard his mother gasp, felt a powerful grip on his neck, and saw the fork with the fat on it moving toward his mouth. He tried to turn his head away but couldn't. He felt the tines of the fork stabbing at his lips.

"Eat your food, boy," his stepfather hissed. "Eat your food."

He felt the sharp press of fingers squeezing his nose closed so that he'd be forced to open his mouth to breathe. He resisted as long as he could, his eyes riveted on his mother, who watched like a stunned animal, horror and helplessness combined in her expression. Then he finally had to gulp in air. With it came the large glob of fat.

"Swallow it, boy. Swallow it or you'll answer to me later."

Sidney felt himself gagging. The grip on his neck tightened. He felt the slimy mass of fat in his mouth. He made retching sounds, certain that he was going to throw up. He reached for his napkin.

"Don't spit it out," his stepfather said. "And it's no use throwing up. You'll just have to eat another piece."

Sidney couldn't bear the taste of it. The texture was repulsive. He couldn't bear the thought of what it was and where it had come from. Most of all he couldn't bear what his stepfather was doing to him, forcing him to submit against his will. The pain he felt in his neck was now acute. Tears welled in his eyes and he fought to keep them back so he wouldn't have to cry in front of them. He would show no weakness. Devers squeezed harder. He swallowed the fat.

"Good," Devers said, letting go. "Now for another one."

Sidney slid off his chair, evading his stepfather's clutches, and ran from the room.

"Come back here, boy!" Devers shouted as he reached out to grab him.

"Richard!" The single word from his mother's lips,

and the fury with which she yelled it, were enough to stop Sidney's stepfather from going after him. She tried to form the words, to shape what she'd say next to express her outrage, but there were no words, just anger, and fear. She wanted to curse the man. She wanted to take her son and leave. But she had no place to go and no money to support them and no skills that would provide her with a decent job. She was afraid and she hated herself for it. She knew that with her outburst she'd brought Sidney and herself nothing but more grief.

2

The Topic of Conversation

Even with his door closed and his head under the pillows, even with his fingers in his ears, Sidney could hear the booming of their voices. Even with his eyes clamped shut, he could see them in their bedroom, his mother doing her best to find courage, his stepfather's venom too much for her from the start.

"How can you be so cruel?"

"He has to learn how to be a man!"

"What kind of man?"

"He has to be toughened up or he'll amount to nothing!"

"He's just a boy!"

"What happens now is what matters later!"

"It's always Sidney! It's never William! I've never heard you say a harsh word to him!"

"I had my say with William when he was younger. I don't have to say anything now."

"Sidney's shy. He's different."

"I'll say he's different. With that head he's a freak."

"How dare you say that!"

"He's Melonhead and he'll always be Melonhead and he'd better get used to it. He's going to have a hard time. He's going to have to fight."

"He can't help his head."

"His head's not going to help him."

"He has other qualities. He's very smart."

"His teachers say he's lazy."

"He's sensitive."

"He's soft. He's spoiled. You agreed when we got married that I'd be a father to your son and you'd be a mother to mine."

"I've kept my end of it."

"And I haven't?"

"I didn't say that. Why do you always have to be so hard about everything?"

"You can't keep babying him."

"You can't keep bullying him."

"What choice do I have? It's in his blood, Meredith. He has bad blood. His father's blood."

"He's got my blood, too."

"It's the blood of failure. Passed from father to son. It has to be dealt with before it's too late. He barely gets by in school. He's antisocial and defiant of authority."

"He gets distracted."

"He stays in his room and reads and daydreams. If something isn't done, he'll end up like that bum you married down there in Los Angeles. Do you want your son turning out like that?"

"Leave him alone. Leave my son alone."

"Or what? You'll take him and run? Where will you go, Meredith? Who will have you? Your mother? I don't think the old witch would let you in her house. She can't stand you. You can't support yourself. Nobody will hire you. You can't do anything. Without me, you and your precious son would starve."

"How can you say that? What's wrong with you?"

Then Sidney heard the muffled scream when she was hit. It cut into him like a dagger, right down to the hilt.

"The next time you raise your voice to me when I'm teaching your son a lesson," he heard Devers say, "remember how that felt. Next time keep your mouth shut."

Sidney wanted to save his mother. He wanted to kill the man who was hurting her. His rage was boundless and so was his fear. He was ashamed of himself because all he could do was hide his face in his hands and cry.

The Way It Is

Sidney didn't come to the table for breakfast the next morning. He couldn't. He wouldn't. He wasn't capable of looking at his stepfather without reacting in some way that would get him into deeper trouble. His mother told him he could stay in his room. She had a welt under her left eye where Devers had hit her. She smiled when she saw him looking at it and told him she'd had an accident and that she was all right. When she left he opened *David Copperfield* and disappeared into its pages, looking for escape, and ultimately encouragement. He wouldn't take a relaxed breath until he heard his stepfather leaving for work.

"I'll see you tonight, boy," Devers yelled from the bottom of the stairs. "I'll see you at dinner."

Then it was his stepbrother's turn. "Hey, Melonhead," William yelled up at him. "The bus is here, Melonhead."

"Sidney's not feeling well today," Meredith said as she came up behind William. "He's not going to camp."

"Nothing a little fat won't cure—right, Melonhead?" William yelled on his way out.

"It would be nice if you didn't call your stepbrother that name," Meredith said.

"What? Melonhead? Melonhead doesn't mind being called Melonhead. Ask him."

"It hurts his feelings."

"What feelings?"

Sidney heard the door slam shut, then heard his mother's footsteps as she made her way to his room. She came in without knocking. She always did. Why wasn't he entitled to some privacy?

"They're gone," she said. She sat next to him on the bed and sighed, looking lost, as much a child in her helplessness as her son. "You have to go to your father's for a while," she said, summoning what strength she could. "You can't stay here the way things are." Her voice broke. Her heart was already broken. "I'll take care of it. You'll come back and everything will be all right. You'll see."

He packed his green canvas duffel bag expertly. This wasn't the first time he'd been shipped unexpectedly from parent to parent. Ordinarily he spent the school year with one and vacations with the other, then switched. Sometimes he wondered why he bothered unpacking at all.

On the bottom of the duffel bag he put his good shoes. Into them he stuffed four pairs of balled socks. He rolled a pair of jeans and put them on top of the shoes. He rolled a long-sleeved shirt and put it in, then three T-shirts, three pairs of jockey shorts, a faded University of Washington "Huskies" sweatshirt, and his bathing suit. On top of all that he put his ditty bag, which contained his toothbrush, toothpaste, and deodorant, which he usually forgot to use, and his hairbrush. A notebook, two medium-tip ballpoint pens, and *David Copperfield* completed the task.

When he was done, he looked about his room. There were posters of ski scenes on the walls. There was a hiking-in-the-mountains poster. There were posters of famous athletes suspended in moments of greatness. None of them interested him. There was nothing in the room to suggest that Sidney T. Mellon, Junior, was its inhabitant. Sidney wasn't at all sure that he owned anything or that he wanted to. If you had something, it could be taken away. He understood that. If you let yourself care, you got hurt.

Meredith backed her car out of the garage, and Sidney swung his duffel bag into the backseat. He climbed in next to her, and they drove off. He looked at the house that his mother had lived in since she'd married Richard Devers and felt nothing but relief to be leaving it. As they drove out of the neighborhood of small, neatly kept houses and yards, he felt a great weight lifting from his shoulders.

Going south, they passed the mall where his mother did most of her shopping. They passed the university. He could see that the "big one" was out. Mount Rainier. The jewel of the Northwest. They passed Lake Union as a seaplane lifted off the water and banked north. Once Sidney and his mother had rented a kayak and spent the afternoon on the lake, paddling among the houseboats and ships. They'd raced seaplanes taking off. Afterward they'd gone for ice cream and he remembered his mother laughing and he felt a lump in his throat thinking about what would happen to her for helping him escape from his stepfather. He wanted her to escape with him, but he wouldn't say so for fear of upsetting her. He didn't want to get involved in his parents' lives. He couldn't afford to.

He kept his lives with his mother and father completely separated in his mind. His life was compartmentalized that way. In the six years since he'd been journeying back and forth between Seattle and Los Angeles, he'd never once mentioned the name of one in front of the other. It was a minefield that had to be navigated daily.

The Space Needle loomed large. The flanks of downtown's skyscrapers gave way to the tunnel beneath the Convention Center, which straddled the highway like a giant saddle. They passed the huge Boeing facility, with its rows of freshly painted, brand-spanking-new jetliners sitting like gooney birds waiting for delivery. His stepfather worked there. Sidney thought about his father and wondered what kind of greeting he'd receive when he showed up unannounced.

Meredith changed lanes. She pondered her husband's reaction to Sidney's leaving. He'd be angry, but she hoped it would pass quickly. Without Sidney around to upset him, he'd calm down. William would sleep over with a friend. They'd have a few nights alone. Her husband would bend a little. She was convinced of it.

They sped on toward the airport and not a word passed between them. In his mind, Sidney was already gone.

Time to Go

She paid for his ticket with a credit card, then took
him to the newsstand. He settled on a package of
hard candy, assorted flavors, which he jammed into
his windbreaker pocket. When he went through the
security gate, he set off the alarm and had to stand
with his legs apart and his arms away from his body
while the guard waved his metal-detecting wand up
and down and around him. He wondered what it
would be like to fly from Seattle to Los Angeles
without having his body scrutinized. It was his belt
buckle.

They moved through the sea of people, past bars
and bagel shops and an espresso stand. They passed

the men's room, which Sidney did not have to use, despite his mother's entreaties to go now so he wouldn't have to go on the plane because she wanted him to stay strapped into his seat for the entire flight so he wouldn't hit his head on the ceiling if they encountered sudden turbulence. They passed gate after gate of flights arriving and flights departing until finally they reached his.

They sat waiting, ignoring the television monitors that spewed forth the news of the day whether you wanted it or not.

Meredith studied her son with cautious glances. He was so young, so small a person to be traveling alone. How often he'd done it. She wished that he didn't have to carry the burden of his head, then promptly scolded herself for being judgmental. He was who he was and she loved him. He'd be all right. She wouldn't allow herself to believe otherwise. She wished her life were different. She fantasized about the two of them living in an apartment. She'd work at Nordstrom's. Sidney would have friends because he'd be in one place all the time and go to the same school every year. She'd loused up her own life and knew it. She didn't want her son to pay the price. She was afraid for him but didn't dare say so for fear she'd make him afraid for himself. She didn't want him to live a life like hers.

Sidney felt his mother's glances and accumulating edginess. It would be like all the other times they'd said goodbye. He could already feel the sadness and inevitable guilt that would accompany the moment. He was leaving her to face the music.

She gave him two hundred dollars in fresh new twenty-dollar bills. He stared at them in wonder. He'd never seen so much money.

"Don't tell your father you have this," she said. "He'll borrow it." She smiled an involuntary smile at the thought of Sid. She'd never fallen altogether out of love with him.

"It's for emergencies. For just in case."

He saw the unhappiness in back of his mother's smile.

"Put it away now," she said. "You don't want any-one to know you have it. Put it in a safe place when you get there. It's okay to spend some of it on fun."

He folded it carefully and put it in his wallet, where it joined forces with his two library cards, his ID, which had his Seattle address on one side and his Los Angeles address on the other, and a fortune from a fortune cookie that read: "You are in your own way, stand aside." The money made his wallet bulge, and it felt huge when he stuck it back into the front pocket of his jeans. It felt like something extra to worry about, a responsibility he wasn't sure he wanted. He turned and watched a plane take off, its nose leaving the ground, then the rest of it hurrying to catch up as it became airborne.

"I would have told your father you were coming," she said, "except then he'd have made some excuse not to take you. If you just show up, he won't have any choice. He won't mind once he sees you. I'm sorry it has to be this way. You have to make him understand why you can't be here right now."

He nodded.

"I hope you understand that all of this has nothing to do with you. I mean, it's not your fault. None of it. I never want you to think it's because I don't want you."

"I don't think that," he said, squirming in his seat.

"You don't know if something is going to work out before you try it. I meant to stay married to your father. I meant for you to have a normal home like a regular kid."

He hated it when she talked like this. It was too personal. It made him feel like he was learning something that was none of his business.

"Your stepfather means well," she said. "He tries to do his best. He's had a lot of stress on the job and he's worried about you turning out all right. It's a hard life, Sidney. You have to be strong."

Sidney felt bad for his mother. He wished her life

were happier. He wished she didn't cry so much. He wished, he wished, he wished. But wishing didn't do him any good, and there was nothing he could do to help her.

"Will you call me when you get there?"

He nodded. She always asked. He always did.

"You'll come back before school starts," she said. "You know it's your turn to go here this year."

He nodded. He knew his schedule better than anybody.

"You'll come back in a week or so," she said.

He nodded. He'd come back when he was told to.

His flight was announced. She stood. He grabbed his duffel bag. They moved to the gate.

"You'll be all right?" she asked, fingering his jacket.

"I'll be great. You don't have to worry about me."

"But I do," she said. "Always." She hugged him, then kissed him, then hugged him again, and then let him go because he was pulling to be free.

"He's only twelve," she said to the flight attendant who checked his ticket. "Keep an eye on him, please."

The flight attendant said she'd do just that. She rubbed Sidney's head, which was another thing he hated, then looked at him closely. He watched her expression jump forward, like a race car shifting gears, from studied indifference to alarm to amazement when she realized how big his head was. How round it was. How red it was. He moved through the doorway, hoping she wouldn't touch him again.

Meredith watched her son go, tears streaming down her face, unable to control her despair. Every time he left, she was convinced that she'd never see him again. When he disappeared from her sight, she moved to the wall of glass, hoping for one last look at her son.

He found his row and stood on the aisle seat to wrestle his duffel bag into the overhead compartment. He sat by the window and strapped himself in. As the plane backed away from its gate, he saw his mother searching for him. He waved. She didn't see him. He turned as the plane turned. This time to go forward.

5

You Never Know Who You're Going to Meet

Mount Rainier almost stuck itself into Sidney's eye, it was so close when the jet climbed past ten thousand feet. Bright sunlight bounced off the mountain's glaciers. It looked like the top of the world. All around him was a cloudless, brilliant blue sky that seemed to stretch on forever. He felt empty now, a vessel waiting to be filled. He desperately wanted to know what was going to happen next. He was tired of the constant anxiety caused by not knowing. He was tired of having to spend so much of his energy on just getting through the day. And he was sick to death of people staring at his head, or trying to sneak looks at it, the way they'd been doing ever since he got on the plane. The way they always did no matter where he was.

He wondered what it would be like to stay up here forever, suspended in space and time. Free from all the laws of science. A self-contained life-form. A self-sustained existence. The plane bounced and rattled. He saw faces tighten and hands grab at armrests. It bounced again, then returned to its even-keeled drone. He wasn't afraid of flying, just tired of it.

"Heading home or visiting?"

Sidney looked across the empty middle seat at the man sitting on the aisle. "Visiting," he said.

"I'm heading home," the man said, smiling, the ends of his bushy mustache shooting upward. He stuck out his hand. "I'm Bernard Livingstone."

Sidney shook Bernard Livingstone's smooth hand. "My name is Waldo Smeely," he said.

"Well, Waldo, I've been away ten days on a selling trip and I can't wait to get back. Miss my family. Nothing matters like family. Who you going to visit?"

"My uncle," Sidney answered. "He lives in Beverly Hills. He's a movie producer."

"Really? No kidding? What's his name? I might have seen one of his movies."

"Chester Smeely," Sidney heard himself say. "You probably never heard of him. He makes cheesewad horror movies."

"Maybe I've seen them on TV," Bernard Livingstone said. "I watch a lot of cheesewad movies on late-night TV when I'm on the road." He smiled nervously. The kid's head was disconcerting.

"His last one was about a vampire who gets trapped in the Arctic Circle during the summer, when it never gets dark. He tried to make the vampire sympathetic by having him slowly waste away, but I don't see how you can feel sorry for anybody who sucks the blood out of people. I don't care how sick they are. It was called *Blood on Ice.* I think it went directly to videocassette."

"I'll look for it," Bernard Livingstone said without much enthusiasm.

"My uncle takes me to the studio with him and I get to meet movie stars and have lunch in the cafeteria and watch whatever they're filming," Sidney said, wondering where the conversation would lead. "I've met Tom Hanks and Jack Nicholson and Arnoooold and Julia Roberts."

"You know Julia Roberts?" Bernard Livingstone was more than a little interested.

"Oh, sure," Sidney said casually. "She's very nice. She rubbed the top of my head." He saw Bernard Livingstone look at the top of his head, then saw his eyes working their way down across his face, widening as they took him in.

"I'm twelve," he continued. "August fifteenth is

V-J Day." He wondered why he'd brought that up. "That's the day we celebrated the Japanese surrender in nineteen forty-five. That was nine days after the first atomic bomb was dropped on Hiroshima. Six days after the second bomb was dropped on Nagasaki. I don't think there should be any atomic bombs."

"You're a bright young man, Waldo," Bernard Livingstone said, taking a last look at Sidney's head before turning back to his laptop computer. It must be some sort of genetic disorder, he thought.

"I'm not really bright," Sidney said. "I just know a lot of things that interest me."

Bernard Livingstone shook his head. The boy was weird. "It was nice talking to you," he said.

Sidney, relieved that the conversation was over, turned his attention back to the world outside his window. The color of the ground had turned from green to brown. He wondered why he made up names and stories. He wondered where they came from. Sometimes he could go on and on, telling the entire story of a character who only a moment earlier had come to life and acquired a name. He'd be Waldo Smeely until he walked off the plane, then Waldo Smeely would be no more. Gone off to his great reward. Never to be heard from again. That was one of Sidney's few rules in life. He couldn't use the same character twice. He dozed off, hypnotized by the drone of the engines.

He shook himself awake as the plane banked west. The announcement came that they'd be landing soon. They passed over the San Fernando Valley, a landscape stamped with grid after grid of streets and houses and shopping malls. Now the air was brown. They crossed the Santa Monica Mountains. Malibu was down there, the beach and the Pacific Ocean. They flew the loop that took them downtown, then back west to the airport. They came in over the freeway, bounced once, then steadied. The tires screeched. The engines went into reverse thrust. Sidney assumed his Los Angeles identity.

Casa Hernandez

He took the van from the airport. It was cheaper than a taxi and slower. He wasn't in a hurry. He sat all the way in the back and had the seat to himself.

The man in front of him yelled into his cell phone. "I don't care. Sue me if you want to. Better yet, I'll sue you. I'll take you for everything you've got. You won't have any underwear left when I get done."

The woman sitting next to the man who was yelling was reading *The Wall Street Journal* and making little hissing sounds of disapproval between her teeth. To which the man on his cell phone was completely oblivious. But the hissing sounds annoyed the driver, who was trying to listen to a talk show on his radio. He kept turning up the volume and glaring at Sidney in the rearview mirror, convinced that the round-headed boy was the culprit. The ride went like that.

Sidney studied the woodpeckerlike oil rigs as they made their way through Baldwin Hills. Up and down the little rigs went, like they were drinking the oil out of the ground instead of pumping it. The great basin of Los Angeles came into view. He would be the last passenger dropped off. They'd stop twice in Beverly Hills, home of the once-famous producer of cheesewad horror films Chester Smeely, then West Hollywood, his destination.

When he arrived at Casa Hernandez, he paid the driver, then checked the building directory and discovered that his father had changed apartments since the last time he was here. He rang the bell, but Sid wasn't home. Why would he be? It was afternoon and he was at work and he wasn't expecting his son. Sidney sat on the steps of the complex and waited, alternately apprehensive about his mother's predicament and his father's greeting. A police car passed, and Sidney thought he saw the cop in the passenger seat do a double take. An ambulance siren caromed off apartment building walls a block away. Finally, Mr. Hoover, a bald man who snapped his fingers when he walked, let Sidney in. Mr. Hoover published a newsletter about famous area cemeteries and the famous people who were buried in them. Mr. Hoover lived next door to his father's former apartment. He looked at Sidney with open disapproval, as he always did when he saw him. Mr. Hoover acted like he owned the place.

"Sid didn't say you were coming," Mr. Hoover observed as they made their way into the large center courtyard that was the heart of Casa Hernandez. It had been built in the fifties and looked like a fancy motel with a lot of Spanish tile. "Wait for your father out here," Mr. Hoover said, taking a final look at Sidney's head, which, no matter how many times he saw it, continued to amaze him.

"I'm only visiting," Sidney said, as he always did. He watched Mr. Hoover walk off, fingers snapping, then rolled a chaise longue under a palm tree to get some shade, checking first to make sure that there weren't any coconuts getting ready to drop on his head. He worried about such things. He looked at the pool and cabana and volleyball court and barbecue pit, then settled his gaze on the two young women in bikinis who were sunbathing. The backs of their tops were unfastened and their bodies glistened with oil and they weren't that much older than Sidney. Late teens, early twenties. He felt a stirring somewhere deep inside. When they looked up, he looked quickly away, feeling vaguely uneasy.

Afternoon turned to evening, and the pool area

began to fill as the smorgasbord of people who called Casa Hernandez home filtered in from work. Voices rose in animated outbursts of exuberance. It was Friday. The weekend was upon them. The good times were about to roll. The cabana was opened, and cold beer and munchies appeared. Music poured forth from speakers hidden in the palm trees. Later, when it was dark, their fronds would glow in the soft haze of colored lights. Laughter floated in the air. And Sidney T. Mellon, Senior, finally came home.

7

Father and Son

"Hiya, pal," Sid said, smiling his big smile, acting like it was the most normal thing in the world to find his son sitting under a palm tree at Casa Hernandez. He didn't want the kid to feel bad. The kid had enough working against him already. What was he doing here?

Sidney jumped up too quickly, lost his balance, and fell back into the chaise with a grunt. He heard laughter. He didn't look but was certain it was directed at him. He pushed himself up again and this time found his feet. It always startled him to see his father when he'd been away for a while. Sid was magazine-cover handsome, in a faded kind of way, and it never seemed quite possible that the man in front of him was his father.

"When did you get in?" Sid asked, cuffing him lightly on the shoulder.

"This afternoon. I haven't been waiting long."

"You look good, pal."

"You look good, too, Sid." Sid was what Sidney called his father. It was what Sid preferred.

"It's good to see you, pal." Sid grabbed the duffel bag, and Sidney followed him into the entrance that was designated in scrollwork above the door "Valencia."

Sid decided not to ask his son why he was here. He wouldn't call Meredith either. Obviously something was going on. He didn't want to know what. He'd let the kid stay a week or two, then send him back. He was in the midst of his own crisis. His job at Ragnor's House of Fine Carpet wasn't going anywhere, and he was increasingly concerned about his age, which was thirty-eight. His hair was starting to thin, and he was getting weary of the hour and a half he had to spend at the gym every other day. He had maybe a couple of years left before he started looking his age. Then what? He was terrified of ending up old and alone in a place like Casa Hernandez.

Lushly orchestrated music filled Sidney's ears as he

followed his father to the elevator. The corridors were lined with muted murals of rolling hillsides and orange groves. The elevator walls were mirrored.

"How was the flight down?" Sid asked. He had a very hard time making small talk with his son. He couldn't figure out why.

"I came on the bus," Sidney said for no reason at all. He wondered where it would lead.

Sid was surprised. Why the bus? Maybe Meredith was having money problems. He looked down at his son and wondered about him. He didn't understand the boy at all. And where had he gotten the head? Not from his family. He realized that he was staring and that Sidney was staring back. He smiled quickly and started to rub his son's head, then remembered not to.

"It's pretty much the same as the other one," Sid said as he let Sidney into his apartment.

Sidney took a fast inventory. The aquarium was there, and the fish looked to be the same, although he couldn't tell one goldfish from another. The same dozen books were on the shelf unit. The TV was on its table with the VCR. The furniture was pushed close together because the room was smaller.

"It only has one bedroom," Sid said. "The carpet business hasn't been so good. I work on commission. It's only temporary. The couch opens up. It's as good as a bed."

"Where's my stuff?" Sidney didn't see a trace of himself anywhere. Not that there had been much. A few books. Some clothes.

"In the storage room," Sid answered quickly, relieved that Sidney wasn't going to make a big deal out of his diminished circumstances. "We'll get it out in the morning. I'll make room for your clothes in my closet. We'll do great, you and me. The good life."

Sidney shrugged. "That's okay," he said. He thought about unpacking and decided not to. He'd live out of his duffel bag for a while and see what happened.

He stood in the doorway to the bathroom watching Sid shave his day-old beard. "There's not much in the fridge," Sid said, pulling the razor against the grain on his neck. "You can call out for pizza. Or Chinese food. Whatever you want. It's all on the speed dial. You can fax your order. You can fax anybody you want to. You have a pal up there with a fax?"

Sidney shook his head.

"How about E-mail? I'm on the Internet. You could E-mail somebody. I've been chatting with a lady in London recently." He looked at Sidney's reflection in the mirror and winked.

Sidney winked back. Sid grinned. Sidney grinned back. Sid started working on his chin. Sidney figured he'd have twice as much to shave when he grew up. He found the thought discouraging.

"What do you think?" Sid asked when he presented himself to Sidney. He was wearing an earth-tone suit that draped splendidly on his spare frame. His hair was slicked back, and he gave off a musky scent. "It's almost an Armani. The suit. Excellent workmanship. Nine hundred bucks. How's it look?"

"Like a million, Sid," Sidney said. "You look like a movie star."

"Yeah, that's what I feel like." Sid showed off a full set of straight white teeth. "A movie star." He pulled out a small wad of bills and gave Sidney twenty. "Call out for something. There's good TV on tonight. You can go pay-per-view. You know where the video rental place is. The extra key is on my bedside table. I don't know what time I'll be back. I wouldn't go out if I hadn't already made the date. You don't stand a lady up at the last minute. Look, I didn't know you were coming."

"I'll be all right," Sidney said. "Stay out as late as you want."

"Could a father have a better son? Give me five."

Sidney slapped his father's open hand, then let Sid slap his back.

"Keep the change," Sid said as he went out the door.

8

Home Sweet Home

The telephone rang once at the other end. Please don't let him answer it. It rang again. Please. Then a third time.

"Hello?" It was his mother.

"I'm here," Sidney said, allowing himself to breathe.

"The flight was all right?" she asked. "No strange people tried to talk to you?"

"Nobody talks to me," Sidney said. "Not for very long anyway."

"You're settled in okay? Your father didn't give you a hard time about being there?"

"Everything is fine. We're going to a movie tonight. I just wanted you to know I got here okay. I have to go."

"Who's that on the phone?" It was his stepfather's voice in the background. "Is that Sidney?"

"Don't tell him it's me," Sidney pleaded.

"It's Sidney, dear," he heard his mother say to Devers.

He thought about hanging up.

"I want to talk to him," he heard Devers say.

"No!" Sidney yelled. "I don't want to."

"Your stepfather wants to talk to you," his mother said.

Devers got on the phone. "Hello, son," he said. "I want to talk to you about something that's been on my mind. Something that will be good for both of us."

Sidney's stomach churned.

"I want to adopt you, Sidney. That's what it comes down to. I've already talked it over with your mother. She thinks it's a fine idea. I want to be your father in every sense of the word and I want you to be my son. You'll be Sidney Devers."

Sidney was struck dumb.

"What do you think of that idea?"

"I have a father," he managed to say.

"I'll get him to agree," Devers said, "and then I'll be your legal father. It will make us a real family. William will be your real brother."

Panic swept through Sidney's body like a riot breaking out at a World Cup soccer match. Sid would never agree. Would he?

"As soon as you start school, I'm going to come down there and work things out with him. Your mother wants to say goodbye."

He heard his stepfather's voice as the phone was passed back to his mother. "He has no appreciation for what I'm trying to do for him. He never even said thank you."

"Isn't that nice, Sidney dear?" his mother said, her voice almost maniacally cheerful. "Your stepfather, your father really, because that's how he feels about you . . . we had a long talk when he got home from work. At first he was upset that you were gone. He thinks all this going back and forth is no good for you. He wants you here all the time and so do I."

"I have to go now," Sidney said.

"Call me tomorrow."

"No." Tomorrow was too soon. "I'm too old to call you every day. I'll call you next week."

"You're sure you're okay?"

"I'm fine."

"Next week then." He could tell by the sound of her voice that she didn't like it.

"Promise me you won't call me before that," he said.

There was a long silence. "Okay," she said finally.

"Okay," he said.

"I want you to come back now," she said. "Tomorrow."

"I just got here."

"What's the point of putting it off if you're coming back anyway?"

"I already unpacked. We made some plans."

"You'll stay a week," she said. "You'll come back a week from today."

"I don't want to be Sidney Devers."

"Just think about it. Please, Sidney. It would make things so much easier. We'd be a real family. Everything would be different."

"Goodbye, Mom," he said quickly and hung up. He was sweating, despite the air-conditioning. His heart slammed against his narrow chest. Who was Sidney Devers? He barely knew who Sidney T. Mellon, Junior, was. They were trying to steal his identity. The thought of becoming Devers's son was beyond reason. But how could he stop it if it was what Devers wanted? Devers was too powerful. He sat on the floor and rocked back and forth, struggling to rid himself of the demon that occupied his body.

In an hour he'd calmed down enough to realize he was hungry. The last thing he'd eaten was a bag of nuts on the plane. He opened a can of baked beans and ate the contents cold. He opened a can of Sid's beer and took a swallow and spit it out and poured the rest down the drain. He didn't know how anybody could stand the stuff. He clicked his way through seventy channels of television, then watched *Big* on video until the part where Tom Hanks eats the tiny ear of corn. He took the cushions off the couch and pulled out the mattress and made up his bed. He brushed his teeth and stripped to his underwear and turned out the light and tried to find comfort in the dark.

9

A Rock and a Hard Place

"You want to go to the beach, take the bus. You have the pool here if you want that. You know where the movie theaters are. I'm nine to seven at the store, so you'll have to figure it out for yourself."

They were having breakfast. Sidney hadn't slept much. Devers's voice had nagged at him. Sid had come home after midnight. They were sitting across from each other at the kitchen counter.

"I have to work next Tuesday and Thursday nights. And next Saturday. Can't make any money if I'm not there. I've been seeing a couple of different women lately, so I'll be going out quite a bit. You wouldn't want your old man to disappoint anyone, would you?" He flashed his kid's grin.

"I wouldn't want you to disappoint anyone," Sidney said. He told himself it didn't matter.

"It's not easy trying to make a decent buck and having a life to go with it. I always wanted to be in business for myself. It's the only way to fly. Make my own TV commercials and play them on the local stations. Like Cal Worthington and his dog, Spot, which was before your time. Used cars, appliances, mattresses, doesn't matter. I've averaged a new job every two years. Every one of them has been the same. The printing business, the toy business, the children's jewelry business . . . what's the difference? Now I sell discount carpet. Not exactly what you'd call an exalted profession."

Sidney didn't want to hear any of this. He tried to change the channel.

"If I don't connect with something meaningful soon, I'm going to spend the rest of my life selling somebody else's merchandise. I'll be one of those old guys in yesterday's wardrobe who smells like mothballs. Don't make my mistakes. Find a solid-gold career and stick with it. Find a wife and stick with her. Sometimes I think if I'd put more effort into it, your mother . . . I'll take the brunt of the blame. I didn't take it seriously enough. I don't really want to get into all that."

Sidney gave his father a sympathetic look, thankful that he wasn't going to have to hear more.

He's not a bad kid, thought Sid. He's a good listener. "After breakfast," he said, "we'll go down to the storage room and get your stuff. We'll fix up the living room. It'll be yours. This is going to be okay." Maybe he'd let his son spend the rest of the summer. What was that? Four weeks? He'd work up to it. "You'll stay a week or two. See how you feel?"

"Sure, Sid. Thanks." Maybe he should say something about his mother expecting him back in a week. He could do it later.

"It's not much of a deal, is it? Living here. Hanging out with me."

"It's okay," Sidney said. "I don't mind."

"I guess this is pretty much a one-man situation, this place." Sid took a swallow of his coffee and tasted only its bitterness. He looked and felt miserable. There were puffy dark circles under his eyes. He had a half hour to get his kid's things from storage and himself to work. He was going to be late.

"You don't get a fair shake living with me, Sidney. I'm a lousy father. I'm not cut out for the job. It's got nothing to do with you. With how I feel about you. You're my son. My DNA. Nobody is more important to me. You need things I can't give you. Up there, with your mother, you have a chance."

10

A Matter of Family

An hour later, they drove down Fairfax Avenue, past Fairfax High, where Sidney had always supposed he'd spend half his high school years. But now Devers was trying to take control of his life. That would change everything. They passed produce stands and butcher shops and Canter's delicatessen and CBS and Farmers Market, then turned left on Wilshire Boulevard and headed downtown. He was going back to Seattle. It was what Sid wanted. What difference did it make if he went now or later?

Sidney stared out the window at the La Brea tar pits and wondered what it would be like to fall into the dark, bubbling muck and become petrified.

Preserved for the ages until one day, like mastodon bones, he was dug up by a paleontologist in Pit 91. They passed Hancock Park and journeyed through the part of the city that spoke to a more genteel and graceful time, when tea was served every afternoon at the old Bullocks department store.

Sidney felt no kinship with this city. He had no sense of it. He'd never walked anywhere. No one walked in Los Angeles. He knew it from car windows. Over the years he'd been on the Universal tour, to countless movies, restaurants, the beach, a miniature golf course, stores, school, and the county museum, all without feeling he'd been anywhere real. He felt the same way about Seattle. That was his mother's city, and his stepfather's. He was just a guest in both places. All the apartments and houses he'd lived in seemed like so many hotel rooms. He packed, traveled, unpacked, packed, traveled, unpacked; that was his life.

Sid pulled the car up in front of a hydrant, switched off the engine, and turned to look at his son. "You're sure about this?" he asked. "You don't mind going back now?"

Sidney nodded that he didn't. What choice did he have?

"You could take the plane and be there in a couple of hours. I'm happy to pay for it."

"I like the bus," Sidney said.

Sid shifted in his seat. He was having an unexpectedly hard time with this. "I can see why you like the bus better," he said. "It's an adventure. I wouldn't mind taking one across the country someday. Coast to coast. L.A. to New York, or maybe even Boston. Meet the people who make America great. The real people." He offered his son a smile and got out of the car. He took Sidney's duffel bag from the trunk and set it on the sidewalk. He had to slam the trunk lid down twice to make it stay. "Car's coming apart," he said. "Everything falls apart sooner or later. I'd help you in with your bag, but I'm parked by the hydrant here."

"I can do it," Sidney said.

"I should take the whole day off. We could do something and you could leave tonight. Maybe tomorrow. We could play miniature golf. We had a good time doing that. It would teach that cheapskate I work for a lesson." Sid grinned. "Who am I kidding?" He looked like a kid who was late for school. "I've got to get there while I've still got the job. You can visit me anytime, you know. You're always welcome. Of course, Thanksgiving is pretty much a family-type deal and you'll probably have a better time up there. I'll end up going to Du-Par's. They serve a good turkey plate. Christmas would be good, although I might go skiing. It depends. I'll let you know what's up."

"I should be going," Sidney said.

Sid nodded and handed Sidney two fifty-dollar bills. It would leave him tight for the month but, hey, it was his kid. "This enough?"

"Plenty," Sidney answered, pushing the money into his pants pocket. "Thank you."

"I'll stay in touch this time," Sid said. "I promise." He shifted his weight from foot to foot. He cuffed Sidney lightly on the shoulder. He wanted to take his son in his arms and hold him. "Take care of yourself," he said instead and stuck out his hand.

"Take care of yourself, Sid," Sidney said. He shook his father's hand. He didn't want to let it go.

Sid drove off, honking his horn and waving without looking back.

"You should pay more attention," Sidney yelled angrily after his father. He wiped at his eyes with his shirtsleeve. "You should care more," he said so softly that he could barely hear it himself. He saw people staring at his head as he lifted his duffel bag and made his way into the bus station.

11

A One·Way Ticket

Old. Used. Worn-out. Certainly no amenities to lure the discriminating traveler. No first-class lounge. No bookstores. No shiny gift shops with overpriced T-shirts and ball caps. None of the glitz of the modern airport. It was fine with Sidney.

He found room on a bench and sat with his bag on the floor between his legs and took in the sights and sounds and smells of the cavernous room. People were reading and talking and sleeping and conducting business with ticket agents and crying because somebody they loved was leaving or arriving, it didn't seem to matter which. He heard laughter and saw despair. He saw a young woman who looked so sad he thought his heart would crack open. He saw a man in tattered clothes sitting ramrod straight, a proud, defiant expression set on his face, hoping perhaps that his bearing would spare him the indignity of being thrown out by the cops.

It occurred to Sidney that he ought to buy a ticket. He found the departure board and saw that there was a bus leaving for Seattle within the hour. But he wasn't going to Seattle. He wouldn't go back to become his stepfather's son. He loved his mother but understood that there was nothing he could do to help her and nothing she could do to stop Devers from having his way with him. His father didn't want him. Sid couldn't handle it. Having a kid wasn't part of the program. But if not Seattle and not Los Angeles, then where? There were buses to San Diego and Phoenix and Dallas and Las Vegas and Reno and New Orleans and one that went to Flagstaff, Arizona, then on across the country to New York City.

"New York City," he said aloud to test it. He didn't know much about New York City. He knew that it was, in round numbers, three thousand miles away. On the other side of the country. Facing the Atlantic Ocean. It was as far away as he could think to get.

He studied the ticket counter from a distance to see how it worked. He didn't want anybody asking him why he was traveling alone. He needed a plan. Some kind of cover story. He started asking people if they were traveling to Flagstaff. When he found an elderly couple who were, he asked if they'd mind if he sat next to them on the bus.

"I'm traveling alone," he said. "My mother is meeting me in Flagstaff." He introduced himself. "I'm Nestor Beachnut," he said. "I've been to two weeks of camp on Catalina Island."

They were the MacLeans, and they were transfixed by the sight of Sidney standing in front of them. They said they'd be delighted to have the pleasure of his company on the bus. He thanked them and said he'd be right back after he bought his ticket.

"One ticket to New York City, please," Sidney said to the agent, who stared openly at his head from the other side of the counter. "One way." He stood on his tiptoes to make himself appear taller.

"That's a hundred and twenty-three dollars," the agent said, a shadow of doubt crossing his expression. "Who you traveling with?" He was supposed to keep an eye out for runaways.

"I'm traveling with my grandparents," Sidney said. He turned and pointed at the MacLeans, who waved and smiled. "I have to buy my own ticket with my own money. My dad said so. I made it delivering newspapers." He counted out the money quickly, using the two fifties and the twenty his father gave him and one of his mother's twenties. The agent couldn't take his eyes off him. Sidney knew what he was thinking. Poor kid, he looks like something that stepped out of the comics.

"Will the bus leave on time?" Sidney asked, trying to take control of the situation. "We like Los Angeles, but we're anxious to get home."

"It's on time," the agent said. He gave Sidney his change.

"My name is Nestor Beachnut," Sidney said. "We came out by train and we're going back by bus. I'm writing a paper on the trip for school. It's my summer project. I'm studying America to prepare myself to be President of the United States someday. My generation is going to fix things."

"Good for you," the agent said. With a head like that, the kid couldn't get himself elected dogcatcher. He slid the ticket across the counter. "Leaves in half an hour. Gate nine."

"It was a pleasure talking to you," Sidney said, grabbing the ticket and his change. "Remember the name. Nestor Beachnut."

Sidney gave the homeless man who was sitting ramrod straight ten dollars and told him to get something to eat. He paid three dollars for a map that showed the bus route across the country. He bought a can of orange soda and a package of peanut butter crackers from the vending machines. He sat with the MacLeans and told them about Nestor Beachnut, who it turned out was an aspiring mountain climber. "I do very well at high altitudes," he told them. "My grandfather on my mother's side was a Sherpa. He was with Sir Edmund Hillary and Tenzing Norgay when they climbed Mount Everest." He told them about the expedition his family was planning to scale the summit. "I'm going to be the youngest person in history to reach the top."

As the door slapped shut, as the brakes expelled their relief at being released and the bus at long last pulled away from the terminal and headed east on Route 10, Sidney wondered why he couldn't be a better son.

12

Melons

Route 10 to Route 15 to Route 40 and across the Mojave Desert and Sidney spent almost all of it looking out the window and seeing nothing. He was suspended in time and place. Trapped in a gelatinous universe. A human Lava lamp. He wasn't going anywhere. He was just going. What did he need with time? What difference did it make where he was? He'd eat when he was hungry and sleep when he was tired. He had no appointments to keep. Nothing and no one counted on him being anywhere.

He moved behind the MacLeans so he wouldn't have to talk to them. He'd run out of things to say about Nestor Beachnut. He was tired of Nestor

Beachnut. He'd told them he wanted to sleep. His thoughts took him back to his seventh year of life, to the time when he'd fallen out of a tree and landed on his head. The kids he'd been with had laughed at him. "All the king's horses and all the king's men couldn't put Melonhead back together again," they'd sung, over and over and over. Even the one adult in the group hadn't been able to resist. "How's the old melon?" she'd said. Even the doctor they'd taken him to hadn't been able to resist. "You've got a tough melon there, young man," he'd said. "Not a bit of damage."

Sometimes Sidney thought that his inability to focus on anything for any length of time was the direct result of that fall. Maybe the bang to the head had left him with something slightly less than a full tool kit. He couldn't relate to people, certainly not in any way that seemed to please them. He spent most of his time daydreaming or contemplating or speculating or projecting. He hated being the object of anyone's attention, even for a minute. Somebody was almost always staring at him. He almost always felt like a freak.

Across the aisle, sitting on his mother's lap, a small boy stared at him now. Sidney smiled. The boy's expression remained unchanged. Sidney made a funny face. The boy responded indifferently. Sidney shrugged at their mutual helplessness. The boy's mother whispered that it wasn't polite to stare at people with disabilities. The small boy frowned and continued to stare, leaving Sidney to wonder if he really was some sort of freak. When he was grown, would people still stare? Would he always be Melonhead?

He tried to remember the first time he'd been called Melonhead. He'd been Melonhead at every school he'd ever attended. He'd be Melonhead in high school. He'd be Melonhead in college. He couldn't remember who started it. Maybe it was the doctor who delivered him.

"It's a Melonhead."

Melons have to mature on the vine, otherwise they're not sweet.

The fruit of the *Cucumis melo*, a plant of the family Cucurbitaceae, which is gourds. Native to Asia and cultivated in warm regions around the world.

The true cantaloupe is named for the town of Cantalupo, which is near Rome.

Columbus brought melons to the new world on his second voyage.

The Juan Canary. The Israeli Ogen. The Galia. The French Charentais. The French Cavaillon. The Sharlyn and the casaba and the Crenshaw. Muskmelons. Watermelons. Persians. Honeydews. The Santa Claus. All melons. From the Latin, *melopepo*. From the Greek, *melopepon*. There are melons pretty much everywhere you go on this earth. Sidney knew all this and more because, if he knew anything, it was his melons.

He was sleeping when the bus passed through Needles, California, population nearly six thousand. Where exactly all those six thousand people were was hard to know. You certainly couldn't see them as you passed through. He was sleeping when the bus crossed the Colorado River, which started in the Rockies of northern Colorado, snaked through the high desert country of Utah, then ground its way through the Grand Canyon, where it joined forces with the Little Colorado at Lake Powell, and finally emptied into the Gulf of California. After people got done sucking their drinking and irrigation water out of it, there wasn't much left.

The bus entered Arizona without fanfare. To the south was Lake Havasu City, home of the London Bridge, brought over stone by stone from London and put back together. They passed Yucca, Kingman, Seligman, Ashfork; and Williams. When the bus pulled into Flagstaff, Sidney woke up.

The MacLeans made a fuss over Sidney, insisting on introducing him to their son, who'd come to get them. He thanked them for their help and had to reassure them three times that his mother would show up. "She's always late," Sidney said. "I have strict instructions not to move until she gets here."

He watched them drive off, then made his way to the rest room of the motel where the bus had stopped. He went to the toilet and washed his face and hands. He saw other passengers brushing their teeth and shaving and taking sink baths with their shirts off, and he tucked away the knowledge for the next stop. He had a long way to go.

Sitting at the counter of the restaurant, watching hamburgers and minute steaks and eggs and bacon and hash browns and tuna melts frying in grease that popped and crackled and splattered and filled the air with a sticky mist, still tasting the fat that his step-father had made him swallow, Sidney decided to become a vegetarian. He ordered a peanut butter and jam sandwich on white toast and a root beer. No more meat. He'd never eat an animal again. Nobody could make him. Flesh was flesh. Bone was bone. What difference did it make whether it came from a pig or a cow or your uncle Louie? And who'd want to sit down to dinner and eat a slice of their uncle Louie?

He decided that he wouldn't do anything he didn't want to from now on. He'd eat what he pleased and wear what he pleased and behave as he pleased. It was his life. His mother thought he was in Los Angeles and his father thought he was on his way back to Seattle. He was sitting at the counter of a restaurant in Flagstaff, Arizona. He was on his own. He wasn't bothering anybody and nobody was bothering him. He intended to keep it that way. He wasn't particularly happy about any of this, but he wasn't sure he knew what happiness was anyway. He had no idea what he wanted except to be left alone.

13

Meeting Moses

To the north lay the Grand Canyon. Ahead, as the bus traveled east across Arizona, was Meteor Crater and, after that, the Painted Desert and the Petrified Forest. Sidney studied his map and saw the names of towns that stirred his imagination: Greasewood and Wide Ruin and Many Farms and Mexican Water. He thought he'd come back someday to see what these places were like and what kind of people lived in them. The names smacked of adventure. They sounded like the towns that cowboy heroes rode into once upon a time and cleaned up, then left, moving to the next town that needed their help. Sidney thought he could have been one of those cowboys. Steely-eyed. Unflinching at the prospect of danger.

There was a commotion in the back of the bus. "Get away from me!" a man's voice yelled. "You're drunk."

Sidney stood on his seat and peered over its high back. He saw a tall, very wrinkled old man with flowing white hair moving herky-jerky up the aisle toward him. Behind the old man stood a very large young man with a purple face shaking a big meaty fist. "Stay away from me or you'll be sorry, old man. I don't like drunk Indians."

"We have a problem back there?" It was the driver.

"No, sir," Sidney heard himself say. "No problem."

The old man stopped and looked at Sidney, his head twitching this way and that. His skin was leathery, cracked, like a mud flat baking in the sun.

"You can sit here," Sidney said. Why was he offering? Hadn't he vowed just a few miles back in Flagstaff not to get involved with anybody? Wasn't he going to mind his own business and let other people mind theirs? Maybe the old man was drunk. And dangerous.

The old man had to try a couple of times before he could get his bottom situated squarely in the seat. "The man I was sitting next to," the old man said, his words slightly slurred, "he said I was drunk. He said my breath was bad. I don't drink a drop and I brush my teeth twice a day. I still have the originals to prove it. I'm a hundred and one. I walk funny. I talk funny. Give me a break."

Sidney didn't see any reason not to believe him. Up close he looked at least a hundred and one. And his breath didn't smell bad. It just smelled old.

"The only thing that fella back there got right was the part about me being an Indian. A Native American these days. Moses Longfellow is my name. My mother read the Old Testament and my father read poetry. I have other names, but this is the one I like."

It took him quite a while to say all this, and Sidney had to pay close attention to pick up every word. What with his slurring, every word Moses Longfellow said sounded like it was one long syllable.

"What's your name?" Moses Longfellow asked.

"Ralph Armani," Sidney said.

"Same as the designer."

"We're not related." Sidney stuck out his hand. It took Moses Longfellow a moment to wrap his big mitt around it. Sidney could feel it trembling. "I'm on my way to New York City to study music," Sidney said. "I have a scholarship."

"I'm going to Gallup to get back a piece of turquoise from a pawnshop," Moses Longfellow said. "It belonged to my mother, then to my wife, then to my daughter, then to my granddaughter, and then to my great-granddaughter, and now it's time for my great-great-granddaughter to have it. The man my great-granddaughter was married to ran off and pawned it. These things happen. What instrument do you play?"

"The tuba," Sidney said without hesitation. "It's a greatly misunderstood instrument. You can't have a marching band without one. You need the *oompah-pah*."

"You look small for a tuba player."

"I have a small tuba."

"Maybe the trumpet would be better."

"I like the tuba."

"How about the clarinet?"

"Tuba."

"I saw an all-tuba band once," Moses Longfellow said. "I liked it."

Sidney nodded, even though he'd never seen such a band in his life.

Moses Longfellow looked him up and down. Here it comes, thought Sidney. Something about his head.

"You're young to be going so far by yourself," Moses Longfellow said.

"I'm thirteen," Sidney said. "Almost fourteen."

"The age a boy becomes a man. Are you Jewish?"

"No," Sidney said. "I'm not really anything."

"It's hard not to be anything," Moses Longfellow said. "My mother thought she was Jewish. She thought she was a member of one of the ten lost tribes of Israel. When I was thirteen she wanted me to be bar mitzvahed. My father was Navajo. He wanted me to spend a month in the wilderness by myself, drinking only the water I could find, eating only what I could get my hands on. He wanted me to become one with nature so that I could understand where I came from and where I was going. He wanted me to hear the voices of my ancestors. So I was bar mitzvahed, then I went into the wilderness for a month. The journey of life is marked by rituals, Ralph Armani. It's too bad you're not Jewish. A bar mitzvah is nice. You get presents."

"What happened in the mountains?"

"By the time I came out I could sing with the birds."

What struck Sidney most of all about Moses Longfellow wasn't his age or herky-jerky movements, it was that he didn't appear to give Sidney's head a second thought. Not once. Instead he seemed to look right into his eyes in a gentle and understanding way that made Sidney feel better.

"I lived the entire twentieth century," Moses Longfellow said, "but I never went to school. My mother taught me to read and write. My father taught me about life. My wife, may she rest in peace, taught me about family."

Sidney couldn't imagine somebody living for an

entire century. From one end of it to the other. "You must have seen amazing things," Sidney said.

"I have," Moses Longfellow said. "I've seen sunrises and sunsets and clear night skies filled with shooting stars and comets and eclipses of the sun and moon and thunderstorms that rocked the earth and lightning that lit it and sweet peaceful days with gentle breezes . . . the things my father saw and his father and his father . . . the things the first man who walked the earth saw . . . amazing things." The old man closed his eyes, and a sudden calmness covered his body like a blanket. The twitching stopped. He was at peace. "It's time to remove myself for a while," he said.

"Where are you going?" Sidney asked.

"Wherever I'm taken," Moses Longfellow replied quietly.

"Why?"

"Why not?" A slight smile played across Moses Longfellow's face. "So I can achieve peace in the midst of chaos," he said. "So that I can visit my beginning and my end." In less than a minute he was sleeping.

Sidney wondered where he was going. He wondered if he'd ever get there.

14

To the Rescue

When they got off the bus in Gallup, Sidney invited Moses Longfellow to eat with him. His treat. Reluctantly, the old man declined.

"I have to find my turquoise and get back on the next bus," Moses Longfellow said. "I hope you find what you're looking for, Ralph Armani."

"I wish you were coming with me," Sidney said.

"Then it wouldn't be your journey. This one has to be taken alone, otherwise you won't get there."

"Get where?" Sidney asked.

"Wherever it's taking you," Moses Longfellow said. "You'll know when it's over. I'll tell you something that will help, the most important thing I learned in a hundred and one years. Be yourself."

"Be yourself?"

"Be yourself."

"That's the most important thing you learned?"

"It is," Moses Longfellow said.

"I'll try," Sidney said. They shook hands, and Sidney watched Moses Longfellow walk off, his body wiggling and squirming this way and that, toward the old part of Gallup to retrieve his family treasure. Maybe you can be yourself when you're a hundred and one, Sidney thought, but when you're twelve and you have no idea who you are in the first place, it's not so easy.

In a stall in the men's room of the motel where they'd stopped, Sidney put on clean underwear and socks. He stuffed his dirty laundry into the bottom of his duffel bag, then emerged and stripped off his shirt, which he himself had to admit was getting pretty gamy. He washed his face and neck and under his arms and dried himself with paper towels. He dabbed on a bit of deodorant, put on a clean shirt, brushed his teeth, then went to the restaurant, where he sat at the counter and ordered the spaghettini with marinara sauce, which was both tasteless and filling.

Afterward he decided to go for a walk. The bus wasn't leaving for a half hour, and he needed to move his muscles and work out the cramps and butt pain that had gathered in him like kinks in a garden hose. It was warm and the air felt good and he picked a distant fast-food restaurant sign as his objective, determined to walk to it quickly and return.

He set out and made good progress, thinking as he went about what he'd do when he got to New York City. But the more he thought about it, the more he realized how enormous his problem was. He didn't know a single person who lived there. So he decided not to think about it again until he absolutely had to. Which would be when he got there. That was when he focused on his surroundings and saw her and stopped. She was young, no more than twenty, with short brown hair and a determined chin. She wore a T-shirt and cutoff jeans, and she was staring angrily at the right rear tire of an old wreck of a pickup truck that was partly jacked up off the ground.

"Are you all right, lady?" he yelled, keeping his distance.

"Yes," she shouted back, looking up, startled by the appearance of the strange-looking boy.

Sidney had problems of his own. He certainly didn't need hers. He started away, then turned back. He couldn't help himself. "You don't look okay to me," he said.

"How could I be okay?" she said, kicking at the

flat tire. "I took my boyfriend's truck and he's after me and I don't want anything to do with the snake and now I have this flat tire and I can't get the stupid lug nuts off and I can't afford to pay a garage to do it."

"I can help you," Sidney said. He'd helped Sid change enough flat tires in his young life. He was sure he could remember the drill.

"Really?" she said, surprised.

"Yes," he said.

She smiled and it was a lovely smile, and Sidney smiled back, not the least bit self-conscious about it. She had that immediate effect on him.

"My name is Gladys Winchester," she said.

"Humphrey Hanks," Sidney responded. He checked the spare. It was as bald as a cue ball and low on air.

"I'm a hairdresser," Gladys said.

Sidney sized up the tire to be changed, then rubbed his hands together the way Sid did. He engaged the lug wrench on a nut and pushed as hard as he could. It didn't budge. He kicked it with a grunt. Nothing happened, except the pain that shot up his leg. When the hero rode into town, he didn't complain about a little pain. He kicked again, with a louder grunt, and he kept kicking until the nut finally gave way.

"I went to beauty school in Albuquerque," she said.

He started kicking at the second nut.

"I'm not saying that hairdressing is an art form or anything, but it's definitely creative. It is the way I do it. I have the touch. Everybody says so. I'm gifted in that regard and I'm not going to waste my life doing it here."

Sidney got the old tire off and the new one on, wrestling it into place the way he'd seen Sid do it so many times, using strength he didn't know he had. He secured the nuts, crisscrossing the lug wrench as he tightened them to make sure the tire was on evenly.

"Do you have any idea how resistant to change people can be in a place like this?" she went on. He was more than happy to let her do the talking. Her voice sounded like honey. "I work my hind end off to keep up with what's going on in L.A. and New York and Paris and Milan so I can offer my customers the latest and all they ever want is what they've always had." She stopped to catch her breath and took a long look at Sidney. He didn't seem so weird now that she'd been talking to him awhile. "What about you?" she asked.

"I was visiting my cousin in Los Angeles," Sidney said. "He's an actor."

A look of astonishment spread slowly across Gladys's face. "Hanks? No. Go on. Get out of here. He's your cousin? He couldn't be."

"He is," Sidney insisted. "On my father's side."

"You don't look anything like him," she said, squinting as she tried to see a resemblance.

"Not now I don't," he said, "but when he was my age, he looked exactly like me." Sidney liked thinking he might end up looking normal someday. "It's a family trait."

"L.A. is where I'm going," she said. "How's that for a coincidence?"

"I'm going to New York City," he said.

"Ever since I was a little girl I dreamed of being a hairdresser in Los Angeles. For me, that's the top. But Clyde doesn't understand. He can't see it. He won't even talk about it. L.A. has the best hairdressers in the world, and I'm going to be one of them whether he likes it or not. It's my destiny."

Sidney wondered about his destiny as she talked on about having her own salon someday, about having the most famous movie stars for clients, about having her own line of beauty products. He wondered if he had any destiny at all.

A car screeched into the parking lot, and a wiry young man with the sleeves of his white T-shirt rolled up to reveal large, hard biceps jumped out from behind the wheel and headed for Gladys, who muttered an uh-oh, which prompted Sidney, who was checking the front tires, to stay hidden behind the truck. Clyde was wearing torn jeans, cowboy boots, sideburns, and an angry scowl.

"Where do you think you're going?" Clyde yelled at Gladys, who looked at him defiantly.

"What do you care where I'm going?" she yelled back.

"I care about you taking my truck."

"How else am I supposed to get there with all my things?"

"You're not going, that's how."

"I am too going."

"No way, Gladys."

"No way you're stopping me, Clyde."

"Get in the truck and drive it back to my place." Clyde spit for effect and started for his car.

"No! You're not telling me what to do any-more."

Clyde turned back, and Sidney felt panic washing over him like a river overflowing its banks. He didn't know what to do. Running would draw Clyde's immediate attention, and he wasn't very fast and probably couldn't get his legs to work just now anyway. All that was left was staying, which did not make him happy.

"I'll walk to Los Angeles if I have to," Gladys said. "Nothing you can do will stop me."

Sidney's heart nearly stopped as Clyde jumped up into the back of the truck. He was no more than two feet away, and Sidney was certain that Clyde would see him at any moment.

"Don't you dare, Clyde Warchuck," Gladys yelled as she climbed into the back after him.

"You want to walk, fine with me." Clyde started throwing her things out, her suitcase, then a cardboard box, then another, and all the while she yelled at him to stop.

Sidney stuck his fingers in his ears. He couldn't stand it. He was terrified of loud, angry voices. He wanted to hide, but there wasn't anyplace, except maybe under the truck, which he was considering when Clyde jumped to the ground and Gladys jumped after him. He saw Clyde raise his hand to hit her. He stepped out from the shadows and put himself between them.

"Don't hit her," Sidney said. He couldn't believe what he was doing. Every fiber of his being was telling him to get out of there.

Clyde hit Sidney instead, knocking him to the ground.

Gladys yelled at Clyde to stop.

Sidney felt the pain ripsawing through his jaw. He felt Clyde grab his shirt and lift him from the ground. He saw Gladys pulling at Clyde's arm, then saw Clyde shake her off and cock his fist to hit him again. It froze there as Clyde got his first good look at Sidney's head.

"This guy's got the biggest head I ever saw," Clyde said.

"He's Tom Hanks's cousin and he's just a kid," Gladys said, picking herself up off the ground.

"He doesn't look anything like Tom Hanks," Clyde said, sticking his face in Sidney's.

"Tom used to look exactly like Humphrey when he was a kid," Gladys shot back. "Isn't that right, Humphrey? Didn't he look exactly like you?"

Sidney struggled to find his voice. He was having trouble breathing. His head throbbed.

"Tom Hanks really your cousin?" Clyde asked.

Sidney sucked in oxygen and Clyde's hot breath with it. His words tumbled out with the carbon dioxide. "Yes he is and he wouldn't like it one bit if you hit a woman." This guy is going to kill me, Sidney thought.

"He wouldn't?" Clyde said, for the first time sounding unsure of himself. He let Sidney go.

"It's against everything he believes in," Sidney said, hoping he sounded more convincing than he felt. "Nobody should hit anybody is what my cousin Tom says. But a man who hits a woman is the worst."

"Tom Hanks was Forrest Gump," Clyde said. He walked off a few feet so he could be by himself to think it over. He didn't want Tom Hanks to be mad at him. Forrest Gump was his hero. He didn't like backing down, but he decided to swallow it.

"Take the truck," he said to Gladys. "And don't bother coming back." He turned to Sidney. "Tell your cousin Clyde Warchuck doesn't hit women." He marched to his car, slammed the door shut after him, and drove off with a screech of tires and the smell of burning rubber.

Gladys gave Sidney a big kiss. "You should put some ice on your face," she said. She kissed him again and thanked him for standing up to Clyde. "Clyde can be mean. You have a lot of courage for a kid."

Sidney could feel his heart slowing in his chest. A beat at a time. The anxiety began to drain from his body. It was like the tide going out. They loaded her things back into the truck.

"You need to put some air in that tire," Sidney said. "You need to get a new one."

She nodded. "I'm glad I met you, Humphrey." She smiled, and Sidney took a mental snapshot. She was beautiful.

"I'm glad I met you, too," he said. "Would you mind if I gave you twenty dollars to help you with your trip? I'd give you more, but I need the rest for New York City."

"I could use it. Thanks."

He gave her the twenty and wished her good luck. He said he hoped to run into her again some-day. She said maybe they'd run into each other in

Los Angeles. "It's a big city," she said, "but a small world."

She kissed him again, this time right on the lips. "I'll do your hair for nothing," she said.

Dazed, he watched her climb in behind the wheel and start the engine. It backfired once. He saw her wave as she drove off heading west. He turned to head back and saw the bus in front of the motel and people getting on it, and he started running as fast as he could.

15

A Place to Stay

Rehoboth, Thoreau, Prewitt, Bluewater, Anaconda, Milan, Grants, McCartys, San Fidel, Acomita, Paguate, Cubero, Casa Blanca, Laguna . . . signs on the road, names on the map of New Mexico. They stopped in Albuquerque, which was founded by the Spanish in 1706, if you didn't count the people who were already there, which Sidney certainly did. A fast meal, a final trip to the men's room, a few new passengers, and the bus was on its way again.

More towns . . . Tijeras, Edgewood, Moriarty, Clines Corners, Santa Rosa, Cuervo, Newkirk, Montoya, Tucumcari, San Jon, and Glenrio, then they were in the panhandle of Texas and on to Amarillo, home to a hundred and seventy thousand people or so and many times that number of beef cattle. Amarillo was where Sidney missed the bus. He went for a short walk and came upon a crowd that had gathered to witness the aftermath of an automobile accident. A Cadillac was half buried in a storefront, and the paramedics were carefully extracting the tiny old woman who'd been driving it. Someone made the observation that she was too small to see over the top of the steering wheel. Someone else said that old people should only be allowed to drive small cars. No one was hurt except the old woman, and she seemed mostly to be all right. Sidney could see her talking and nodding her head as the paramedics asked her questions. When he got back to the station, the bus was gone.

"The next bus to New York City pulls in here at six-thirty tomorrow morning," the ticket agent said to Sidney, sucking on a tooth.

"My ticket is good for that?" Sidney asked, his anxiety just barely under control. Sometimes he felt as though life were a tennis match and he was the ball.

"No problem," the agent said.

"Can you recommend a place to spend the night?"

The ticket agent leaned forward and stared at Sidney. "You a dwarf or something?" he asked finally.

"I am," Sidney said.

"You with the circus?"

"I'm a clown," Sidney answered without hesitation.

"I figured something like that," the agent said, pleased with his powers of observation. "Go out the door and make a right. Six blocks down is the Starbright."

Sidney retrieved his duffel bag from the locker where he'd stored it after using the facilities, slung it over his shoulder, and headed down the street. It was hot in Amarillo. Close to a hundred. He was drenched with sweat by the time he reached the Starbright Hotel, which he could tell right away had seen better days. The lobby was dimly lit and its paint faded.

"How much is a room for the night?" Sidney asked the thin, long-faced young man with the bad complexion behind the desk. The man was wearing a shiny blue blazer and a plastic tag that announced his name was Buzz.

"All we have is the single deluxe," Buzz said with a wide yawn. "It goes for sixty-five bucks a night."

"I'm with the circus," Sidney said. "I understand you have a discount for that."

"No discounts."

"Not even for a clown?"

"Not even for the Queen of England," Buzz said.

"How about something cheaper than the single deluxe?"

"The single deluxe is the smallest, cheapest, and only room we have. They're all single deluxes." Buzz stared openly at Sidney's head, his mouth slightly ajar with disbelief. "I could see where you could be funny," he said. He never cracked a smile.

Sidney hefted his duffel bag and retreated to the far corner of the lobby. Using his bag as a shield, he carefully counted his money. He had one hundred and fifty-three dollars and forty-one cents. If he spent sixty-five dollars on a room, he'd have eighty-eight dollars and forty-one cents left. He was only in Amarillo. New York City was a long way away. At this rate he'd have nothing left when he got there. He became aware of the music that was floating out from the cocktail lounge. He heard an electronic keyboard and a woman singing and the steady rhythm of a snare drum being brushed, *swish-swish*, *swish-swish*, and he was drawn to it.

"Sorry, kid, you have to be twenty-one to come in here," the bartender said.

Sidney nodded, but he didn't move. He was standing just inside the entrance to the Observatory Room, which was what the cocktail lounge was called. His gaze swept from the bartender across the tops of the empty tables to the duo performing on the small stage. They were bathed in a soft white spotlight.

"You gotta go, kid," the bartender said. "Now."

"Can't I just listen to the music?" Sidney asked. "Nobody's here."

"Listen outside," the bartender said. He was losing patience.

"But you can hear it better in here."

"Don't give me a hard time." The bartender started out from behind the horseshoe-shaped bar, which shone bright with the luster of endless wipings.

"Why do I have to be twenty-one to listen to music?"

"You have to be twenty-one to be in the room."

"What if I told you I was a clown with the circus?"

"I'd say be a good clown and get out before there's trouble." The bartender grabbed Sidney's arm.

"Give the kid a break, Ernie."

Sidney saw a woman in a long fringed skirt, satin shirt, and cowboy boots, her silky, straw-colored hair hanging loose down her back, a tired smile stuck to her face like lipstick. She came around from the darkness of the other side of the bar. In the Observatory Room's muted lighting, she looked like a beauty queen.

"Come on, Mona, you know he can't be in here," Ernie said.

"He just wants to listen to the music. I'll sit with him. Make sure he stays out of trouble."

"What's your interest?" Ernie let go of Sidney's arm.

"We were all kids once," Mona said, her voice sounding weary. "At least I think we were."

Now that she was closer, Sidney could see that she was his mother's age, or older. She wore a lot of makeup.

"A half hour," Ernie said, "unless somebody comes in before that. Then he's out of here."

"Whatever you say, Ernie," she said. "You're the boss." She turned her attention to Sidney. He was a peculiar-looking boy. So what? She'd stopped paying attention to faces a long time ago.

"What'll you have to drink?" she asked Sidney. "Ernie's got Coke and ginger ale."

"Ginger ale," Sidney said. "Maybe he could put a cherry in it."

She laughed, which made her more attractive, then looked over at Ernie, who was watching them with a careful eye. "Ernie, my love," she said, "a ginger ale with a cherry for my gentleman friend and a tequila and grapefruit for me." Her voice was husky. Sidney liked the sound of it.

"Who's paying?" Ernie wanted to know.

"I am," Mona said, lighting a cigarette.

"That's a switch." Ernie grinned. He was missing a tooth.

"I'm paying," Sidney said. He took a twenty from his pocket and showed it to Ernie.

Ernie looked at the money, then at Sidney. "You're a nervy little kid," he said. "I'll give you that."

Mona led Sidney to a table in a corner. He dropped his duffel bag and sat and turned his attention to the two spotlighted figures on the stage, who'd been playing the whole time.

Mona studied him until he became aware of it. "You really with the circus?" she asked.

"I've just started," Sidney said. "I'm going to be a clown."

She eyed his duffel bag when he shifted his gaze back to the duo. The singer was dark-haired, sloe-eyed, freshly scrubbed, dressed in sequins, and only marginally talented. It was hard to take your eyes off her. She played the keyboard and sang, taking obvious pride in her ability to do two things at the same time. Her partner was another matter. He was gangly and had long hair and a long nose, and he was a terrific drummer. You could see how badly he wanted to cut loose.

"Charlene, she stinks," Mona said. "Armando, he's not bad. But she's got what sells and she'll make it to the big motel lounges on that alone. He should be playing jazz, but he's in love."

Sidney already knew the drummer was good. That

was what had attracted him in the first place. He was keeping the beat with his hands. The drumming sounded like his heart on a good day.

Ernie approached with their drinks and set them on the table along with Sidney's change.

"Thank you, Ernie," Sidney said.

Ernie leaned in and whispered to Sidney, man to man. "Watch yourself, kid." He grinned wolfishly and left.

"Leave him a buck," Mona said. "Always leave something for the people who wait on you. The better they treat you, the better you treat them. That's a rule of life."

Sidney folded a dollar in half the way he'd seen Sid do it, then tucked it under the edge of the ashtray. He stuck the rest of his change in his pocket. He was down to a hundred and forty-three dollars and forty-one cents.

"Mona Lipp," she said, introducing herself, then tasting her drink. "With two *p*'s. It's French. I've never been to France."

"Buster Means," Sidney said.

"So, what's your story, Buster?"

"No story," Sidney said. "I'm on my way to New York City to go to circus school. I missed my bus. It's no big deal. I'll catch the first one in the morning."

"Your parents don't worry about you being out on the road alone?"

"I don't have any parents," Sidney said. He offered her his most sincere smile. His feet didn't touch the floor. He could feel them dangling. He hated that.

"You running away from an orphanage or something?" When he didn't answer, she figured she must be close. Not her problem. "You hang out in bars a lot?"

"Just for the music. It makes me feel better."

"What grade you in, Buster?"

"Oh, I'm not in school anymore. I dropped out when I was sixteen. I'm older than I look. What do you do?"

A half-moon smile formed on her face as she contemplated an answer. She figured him for fourteen at the most. "I work here," she said finally. "People talk to me and buy me drinks."

"Like I'm doing."

"Exactly."

"What do the people who buy you drinks talk about?"

"Themselves mostly. Their troubles. Their dreams."

"I don't like to talk about myself," Sidney said.

"That makes you unusual," she said. "Most people can't stop themselves."

"If all they do is buy you drinks, how do you make money to live?"

"They leave me tips. Like they would for a waitress."

"Just for listening to them?"

"I'm a good listener. I cheer people up. There's too much unhappiness in the world. You spending the night here, Buster?"

"Actually, I'm not," Sidney said. "I was going to ask you if you knew of a hotel that's less expensive than this one."

"No place I'd let anyone I liked stay. Especially a kid."

"I'm not a kid." He turned to applaud the duo, who announced that they were taking a dinner break and would be back later. Where was he going to stay? He'd never slept on the street before.

"What about my place?" Mona said.

He looked at her, his expression a question mark.

"You can stay at my place if you want to."

"Why?"

"I don't know. It just occurred to me."

"I could be a mass murderer or something. You don't even know me."

"And I could boil little boys and eat them for a late-night snack," she said.

"I wouldn't taste very good."

She laughed. "Yes or no?"

"Yes," he said and went to the lobby to wait for her.

16

Mona

Sidney woke as if from a deep trance. Music from the Observatory Room invaded his consciousness, and he remembered where he was. In the lobby, waiting for Mona.

What, he wondered, would his parents do when they discovered he was gone? Would his stepfather be sorry? He didn't think so. Would his mother leave his stepfather? Unlikely. Would his father decide that he really wanted Sidney to live with him? Doubtful. He closed his eyes and imagined himself dead. Everybody who'd ever done him an injustice was at his funeral. They were all crying. He saw it from above as one by one the long line of mourners stepped forward to say how much they missed him and what a wonderful boy he'd been and how, if only they could have another chance, they'd treat him better.

He went to the restaurant and had a piece of coconut cake. It was stale. He washed it down with a glass of water. He returned to his post in the lobby. Sleep slipped up on him again and took him away, and he didn't realize it until Mona shook him gently awake. It was just after ten o'clock.

"A slow night," she said. "Let's go."

She drove them to her apartment at the edge of the city. Sidney looked out the window, preoccupied with Mona and what he was doing, hoping that it wasn't going to lead to some sort of trouble. Mona glanced at Sidney unobserved. If she and the one decent man she'd known in her life had had a kid, he'd be about Sidney's age. He or she. She wasn't sure how good she'd have been with a daughter.

"How old are you really, Buster?" She wanted to draw him out, learn something about him. He'd been tight as a drum since they'd met. "You don't have to answer that," she said, changing her mind. Prying wouldn't help.

"Seventeen," he said. "I look this way because I have Harrison's disorder." Whatever that was. "It's not terminal."

She nodded. "The circus thing, that real?"

"Oh, I'm very serious about being a clown. It's my

life's calling. There are two kinds of clowns, the ones who get the pies in the face and the ones who throw them."

"Which kind are you going to be?"

"I'll get the pie in the face. I was born for it."

"I think everybody should get a pie in the face once a year," she said. "To keep them honest."

"It will be a national holiday," Sidney said. "We'll call it Pie Day. All the people who get pushed around can smush pies into the faces of all the people who do the pushing." He smiled.

She pulled up in front of a small adobe apartment building. "This is it," she said. "Better than the Starbright and cheaper."

He grabbed his bag and they started inside. It looked nothing like Casa Hernandez, but it made him think about his father. Maybe because it looked so sad.

"What'll you have to drink, Buster?" she asked as they entered the most cluttered room he'd ever seen. There was furniture everywhere, and it was all jammed in, leaving only narrow paths to get around.

"What do you have?" He put his duffel bag down next to the door in case he had to run. He still wasn't sure what was going on here. He couldn't think of any reason why a stranger would treat him so well.

"I have grapefruit juice and I have water," she said.

"Grapefruit juice will be fine. Thank you."

She poured him a glass over ice, then made herself a tequila and grapefruit and returned to the living room, where Sidney waited for her, still marveling at how much stuff she'd fit into such a small space.

"I have a lot of junk, don't I?" She started looking through her CDs. "Most of it was my mother's. I got it when she died. I should sell it, but I can't get myself to make the first move. It's not like it has any sentimental value. We didn't get along." She put on Willie Nelson and told Sidney to take a load off. "Sit down if you can find a place to do it," she said.

He moved crablike between a table and a couch and sat and watched as she removed her hair. When she saw the expression on his face, she laughed. "You never saw a wig before?" She rubbed her real hair, which was no longer than a crew cut and turning gray.

"It sure makes you look different," he said.

"Tell me about it." She plopped down into the only stuffed chair in the room, took a sip of her drink, and set it on a table. Then she removed her artificial leg from its socket.

Sidney jumped to his feet and almost fell over. "What are you doing?" he shouted. "Where'd that come from?"

"This thing gets tiresome at the end of the day,"

she said. She rubbed the stump, then pulled her skirt down over it.

"I've never seen one of those before either," he said, curiosity replacing his astonishment.

"Here," she said, holding it out to him. "Try it on for size."

He leaned across the table and took it and examined it carefully. It was soft to the touch and lifelike in appearance, and the foot moved this way and that, almost like a real one.

"Almost as good as the real thing," she said. "I lost the one I was born with in Alaska. Stepped in a bear trap. Snapped it right off. Where were you born, Buster?"

"I don't know," he said, handing her leg back.

"That's like having no identity," she said. "Everybody should know where they're from."

"It doesn't make any difference where I'm from or who I am or how I got here," Sidney said. "I'm Buster Means and I'm going to be a clown. That's all I have to know."

"I was born in Fairbanks. I was brought up in the wilderness. I could fish and hunt and skin an animal when I was your age. Then my father took it in his head to move to Las Vegas and strike it rich. Which was the end of his story. After that I drifted. Reno. Pullman. Spokane. Seattle. San Francisco. Amarillo."

"Amarillo's not so bad," Sidney said. "I've seen lots worse places than this."

"Thank you," she said.

For a fleeting moment he felt the urge to share his circumstances and not feel so alone in the world. But what good would the truth do him? It would only make his life more complicated. Maybe he was just feeling sorry for her. Maybe he was just feeling sorry for himself.

"Everything will be all right," he said, knowing it sounded stupid when he heard himself say it. Not knowing why he said it in the first place.

"Some days I don't know why I bother to get up," she said. "It's just going to be the same as yesterday. Other days I figure, maybe today's the day a surprise is coming. You never know what's going to happen next."

"That's right," Sidney said. "You never know."

She downed the rest of her drink, then pushed herself up onto her one leg. Sidney couldn't take his eyes off the empty space beneath her skirt. She steadied herself.

"Good night, Buster Means," she said. She started hopping toward the bedroom. "There's a pillow and blanket in the closet, if you can get the door open." She nearly lost her balance and giggled, sounding like the twelve-year-old girl she once was. She grabbed

98

the doorjamb to steady herself. "I'm a little bit tipsy," she said.

He moved quickly to take her arm and helped her to the bed. He turned her so she was sitting, then let her go, and she fell over in a laughing heap. He straightened her out on the mattress and got the sheet up over her and the pillow under her head.

"Take my alarm clock," she murmured, already near sleep. "Be quiet when you leave." She started to snore.

He studied her as she lay there, her mouth slightly open, looking her age and more, nearly bald and minus a leg, then bent to kiss her on the forehead.

"Good night, Mona Lipp with two *p*'s," he said, then went off to see if he couldn't get some sleep himself.

17

Moving On

The tar patches on the road were glossy-slick and blistered from the heat. The sun baked the bus like bread in the oven. Past Conway they went, past Boydston and McLean and Shamrock and on across the top of Texas and into Oklahoma.

Sidney slept. He watched the passing landscape, which sometimes seemed like the moon. He got off the bus and on the bus. He ate. He washed up in rest rooms. He slid under the doors of pay toilets, which were the only ones that came close to being clean. He was becoming compulsive about saving money. He read more of *David Copperfield*. He caught people staring at his head. He saw bewilderment in their faces and sometimes hostility before they looked away.

The bus drove on into the night. Some of the passengers turned on their reading lights. Some sat quietly in the dark. The hushed murmur of conversation could be heard here and there. Someone snored in the back. The engine produced a steady, pleasant background hum. All of it blended together into a kind of music, not unlike the night sounds of a swamp with its croaks and chirps. Sidney thought about Moses Longfellow and wondered how his life might be different if he'd had grandparents.

He never knew his father's parents. They were killed before he was born. A tractor-trailer lost its brakes and went out of control, and its tail snaked across the divider like the back end of a conga line just as their car came around the corner. His mother's father just disappeared one day. When she was fifteen. He went off to his job at the electric company on a sunny morning in June and never came back. His mother told him that from time to time money would show up in envelopes postmarked from different places around the country. But there was never a return address and not so much as a single word of explanation. His mother's mother, the one and only Alice, was still very much alive. Not that it did Sidney much good. He'd met her a few times, when he was very young. He'd gone with his parents, when they were still together, to visit her in Rhode Island. He remembered not liking her and understood that she'd felt the same way about him. He remembered that she smelled funny and was loud. She'd turned out to be no more of a grandparent to him than the ones who were dead.

He slept again, weary from the inactivity of sitting hour after hour, drained from the weight of his conflicting emotions about what he was doing. He couldn't turn back now. He'd come too far. He'd go as far as the bus would take him. He'd struggle to keep his faith in an uncertain future. He woke with a start. He stared out the window at distant lights and allowed himself to think about Mona.

That morning he'd stirred from sleep before sunrise, his anxiety about missing the bus making the alarm clock unnecessary. In the dark he thought about asking Mona if he could stay. A big piece of him wanted to. Living with her would be better than what he was running from. He could go to school in Amarillo. It didn't make any difference. Schools were all the same. He could do the shopping for her and run errands. He could get a part-time job. He could make himself plenty useful. He wouldn't ask for much. He didn't need much. But in his twelve-year-old heart of hearts, he knew he had to go. Nothing in Amarillo would change his life for the better. Mona had too many problems of her own.

He'd left a note thanking her. He wrote that he hoped to be back this way again someday and that he'd look her up. Maybe he'd be back with the circus. When he'd left the apartment, just as he was about to close the door, he stopped for a last look. He inhaled its smells, wanting to remember her forever.

Two blocks away he'd found a taxi. The driver was having his coffee and doughnut, and he had to wait. "Never eat and drive at the same time," the driver had said. "You'll live longer." On the ride to the bus station he'd thought about what Moses Longfellow had told him, that he wouldn't know where his journey ended until he got there. It was hard not knowing where you were going.

Standing in line to board the bus, Sidney had seen Mona's car pull up. She'd hurried to him, her face unwashed, wearing last night's clothes, her wig and artificial leg in place.

"I wasn't sure I'd get here in time," she'd said. "Why didn't you say goodbye?"

"I thought you wanted to sleep."

"I wanted to say goodbye is what I wanted." She'd tried to smile but clearly was saddened by his departure. Part of her wanted him to stay. Having a kid in her life might be enough to straighten things out. She'd get a job. She'd be responsible for somebody besides herself. Who was she kidding?

"Good luck," she'd said. She'd handed him a piece of paper. "My address. Send me a postcard. Just one. To tell me how you're doing. Wait until something good happens. I don't want any bad news. I'll put it on the refrigerator so I can see it every day."

"Lipp with two *p*'s," he'd said. "I'll send you more than one."

"No. Just one. I don't want to know after that." She'd handed him the Willie Nelson CD. "Something to remember me by," she'd said. She'd kissed him and run, as best she could, back to her car. Sidney could see she'd started crying.

———

He felt tears stinging his eyes now as the bus crossed into Arkansas and sped on toward Tennessee.

18

Now You See It . . .

"Top of the morning to you," the man said to Sidney as he sat down next to him. "What a grand day it is." The man was small and wiry-hard, a perfectly proportioned bald man who was hardly taller than Sidney himself. He was wearing a blue suit, white shirt, and red necktie, and he was the blackest man Sidney had ever seen. His voice was the strangest. Like some kind of singsong musical instrument. The bus lurched forward. The man turned to Sidney. "How do you do," the man said. "My name is Shamus Flowers."

"Edsel Bellringer," Sidney said.

"That's an unusual name."

"My father named me after the car. He owned one once."

"Ahead of its time, the Edsel. I had a ride in one. Also a DeLorean. They were made in Ireland, you know. That's where I'm from. Dublin. It's a pleasure to meet you, Edsel Bellringer."

"It's a pleasure to meet you, Shamus Flowers," Sidney responded. "My whole family are all bell ringers. One of them is a champion."

"And do you ring the bells, Edsel?"

"I'm tone-deaf," Sidney said, pointing a finger at one of his ears for emphasis.

"I know what you mean," Shamus Flowers said, scratching a spot on his chin. "I can't play a musical instrument. I can't dance. I don't play sports. You don't see bell ringers around much anymore."

"You hardly see any at all," Sidney said.

"Your whole family, how many is that?"

"Fourteen brothers and sisters, Mom and Dad."

"And they all ring bells?"

"They ring bells. They play spoons. They spin plates on rods. Mom and Dad do a knife-throwing act. My brothers and sisters ride unicycles. They all juggle. Except Dad. He lost a hand juggling chain saws."

"Well, every profession has its drawbacks," Shamus Flowers said.

"I agree," Sidney said. He turned to look out the window. End of conversation. No more Edsel Bellringer.

"You have a large head on you, Edsel Bellringer," Shamus Flowers said.

Sidney turned to Shamus Flowers, his heart aching. "I can't help the size of my head," he said. "Please don't talk about it."

"Hard not to notice," Shamus Flowers said, "but I won't talk about it if you don't want me to. Wouldn't do that. Where you headed?"

"That's not funny," Sidney said.

"You've got to see the humor in it, Edsel. First person who laughs at you should be yourself. Takes the sting out of it. The rest won't matter."

"I'm a jockey," Sidney said. "I'm on my way to race in New York."

"Well now, that's interesting," Shamus Flowers said. "Never met a jockey. You're small enough, but that's a lot of wind resistance up there above the neck." Shamus Flowers took a dollar coin from his pocket and started manipulating it across the top and in between his fingers. Sidney couldn't take his eyes off it.

"I bury my head behind the horse's neck," Sidney said. "It works out fine. I'm just getting started. Someday I'll be famous and you'll read about me in the sports pages."

"You'll be reading about me, too," Shamus Flowers said. "In the obituary pages. I'm in the process of dying, you see." He made the coin disappear.

Sidney's system went into immediate overload. Why was he being told this? What was he supposed to do about it? What was he supposed to say?

"I've been traveling around the country to take a look at things. The Grand Canyon. Disneyland. The Watts Towers. You ever see those? Church steeples reaching all the way up to heaven. The man who built those left something behind him. I've been to New Orleans and San Francisco and Taos, New Mexico. Love those sopaipillas. I have prostate cancer." He made the coin appear from behind Sidney's ear.

"I never knew anybody who was dying before," Sidney said. He watched as Shamus Flowers moved the coin slowly back and forth between his palms. "Not to talk to. Are you afraid?"

"I was, but I'm not now. The wee people had a conversation with me." Shamus Flowers turned in his seat so that he was facing Sidney directly. He moved a little closer. He closed one hand over the coin, showed Sidney the empty palm of the other, then closed that one. "Say you knew that you were going to die next Friday at three o'clock in the afternoon. Say a piano was going to fall on you. You'd be worrying about it and carrying on and you wouldn't live a minute of the life you had left doing anything else and come Friday the piano would fall on you anyway. Bam! But say you didn't know exactly when it was going to happen. I mean, everybody is going to die sometime. That's how it works. Why, you'd go to the movies and have something good to eat and buy that new shirt you had your eye on. That's what I'm trying to do, act like I don't know the piano is going to fall on me." He opened the hand with the coin in it, but the coin was gone. He opened the other hand and showed the coin to Sidney.

"Can't you do anything about it?" Sidney asked.

"Not one thing, Edsel Bellringer. Because it has metastasized. As we speak it spreads itself to my extremities and into the basement of my bowels. It rides the great lymphatic highway. It moves through my veins and arteries in a stately fashion, like so many ships passing through the Panama Canal. Metastasiiiiiiiiiiiiiiize." He stretched the word out until it nearly broke in two. "It's from a Greek word. I looked it up in the dictionary." He closed his hand over the coin, blew on it, then opened it. The coin was gone.

"You're not going to die today, are you?" Sidney asked with some considerable concern.

"Not that I know of. Not while we're talking. It's somewhere off in the future. Meanwhile, I'm going to rent me a room in Nashville and have some serious fun." Shamus Flowers stuck his hand into Sidney's pocket and pulled out the dollar coin. "It's yours," he said, giving it to him.

"Thank you," Sidney said, studying it, wondering if he could ever learn to make it disappear.

"Practice," Shamus Flowers said. "Whenever you don't have anything to do, take it out of your pocket and practice."

Sidney unwrapped his peanut butter sandwich.

Shamus Flowers coughed and fell forward into Sidney and removed the wallet from his pocket as deftly as he'd removed the coin. "Excuse me," Shamus Flowers said, recovering from what appeared to be a bout of pain. "I beg your pardon."

"That's all right," Sidney said. He offered Shamus Flowers half his sandwich. "I couldn't eat it all myself."

Shamus Flowers slipped Sidney's wallet into his own jacket pocket with one hand and took the half of sandwich with the other. "Thank you, Edsel Bellringer," he said. "You're a generous young man."

They chewed in silence, unsticking the peanut butter from their teeth and the roofs of their mouths with their tongues, wishing they had something to drink.

Sidney wondered what dying felt like.

19

How Big Is the Universe?

They stood outside the bus station, next to the newspaper machines. For a long time they didn't say anything. They looked about and took in the day and watched the passing traffic. Shamus Flowers shifted his small suitcase from one hand to the other. "It was good knowing you," he said finally.

"It was good knowing you," Sidney said. "I'll practice until I can make it disappear."

Shamus Flowers took Sidney's wallet from his pocket and held it out to him. "Take care, be aware," he said.

Sidney stared at it like it was a foreign object. Then he recognized it as his own.

"Ordinarily I wouldn't give it back, but a man who shares his food deserves a second chance."

Sidney took his wallet and started to open it.

"I didn't touch a thing," Shamus Flowers said. "Good luck with the horses. I'll be looking for you in the sports pages."

"Are you really dying?" Sidney asked.

"As sure as day turns to night," Shamus Flowers said. He turned on his heel and walked off.

"Thank you for giving back my wallet," Sidney yelled after him.

Shamus Flowers flashed Sidney a smile, then continued on his way. There was a bounce to his step.

Sidney looked in his wallet anyway, then put it back into his pocket, determined to be more careful. Still, there couldn't be many people in the world with hands like Shamus Flowers's. He fingered the dollar coin. He studied the front page of the newspaper through the glass window of the vending machine. He half-expected to see his name. SIDNEY T. MELLON, JUNIOR, MISSING, the headline would read. A photograph of his big, round face would be next to it. Where has Melonhead gone? the story would begin. Was he kidnapped? Has he come to a violent end? But he knew he wasn't being looked for. Not yet. Not enough time had passed. His parents thought they knew where he was.

There were a half dozen men in the bus station's

rest room. One was shaving, another was washing. Two were relieving themselves. One was encased in a stall. Sidney stood at the urinal closest to the door, trying to do his business quickly so he could get out of there unnoticed. But they all saw him.

"Hey, kid, where's your keeper?" one of the men said.

"You could shoot baskets with that head," said another.

"Drill a couple of holes in it, you could use it for a bowling ball," a third man chimed in.

They all laughed.

Sidney retreated. He was happy when the bus got under way again. It was the center of his universe, this bus and its smells and sounds; the sneezes and snores and belches and accumulated fragments of conversation that hung in the air like stale cigarette smoke. He was part of the life force of its human cargo. He could be traveling at the speed of light or hardly moving at all. It made no difference. The engine hummed. The tires whined. It was all the same. It made no difference where he was going. Until he got there, he was here. This was his home. It was all he had.

He imagined himself soaring through the sky, flying with the eagles, his arms extended like wings, a human glider riding the wind currents with gleeful freedom. Then he swam with the whales in their oceans, an honorary member of the universal pod, the bridge between their world and his. He made a speech and everybody heard it and people stopped killing whales and everything else, including each other. In a flash of insight he saw that everything alive was of equal value. And just as clearly he understood that what lived also died. Including Shamus Flowers. Including himself. Even the planet upon which he was presently traveling. Each thing in its time. That was the way of things. Everything comes to an end. Someday, in millions or billions of years, Earth would become an inanimate object floating through an indifferent galaxy, a frigid, empty wasteland left barren of life and all knowledge of human existence.

So what meaning did life have, then? Why bother? So what? Why was Shamus Flowers going to live with as much energy and passion as he could right up to the very end? Life is what you have when you have it, Sidney thought. He wanted to live it with passion. He wanted it to matter. But how could he, with his head and his family? How could he ever amount to anything?

20

The Offer

The bus headed east across Tennessee, past Lebanon and Cookeville and Harriman and Oak Ridge to Knoxville. Sidney watched the changing flow of passengers and the passing landscape. He listened to the twang of new accents. At each stop he stretched his legs and used the facilities. The hours passed, one after the other, and he was hardly aware of time at all. They headed northeast on Route 81. They entered Virginia. Sidney slept. He dreamed. He was a baby. Naked. Living in a hole in a wall, his little knees scrunched up against his chest. He couldn't move. People came to free him, but no one could. Like Excalibur, he waited to be drawn from his prison. He wanted to run through a tall field of grass. A crowd gathered. They gaped at his head. They talked baby talk, which he couldn't understand. He pleaded for help, but no one understood him.

"Get me out of here," Sidney screamed in a language that sounded like babble. "Get me out."

"Are you all right, child? Are you all right?" It was a woman's voice. It was filled with concern. He felt himself being shaken lightly. He was being rescued. He was lifted from the hole. He came awake. He was looking into a sweet, kindly face. The woman smiled. The skin crinkled around her eyes and mouth.

"You were having a nightmare," the woman said. She was gray-haired and in her sixties and wore a simple floral-print dress. She spoke softly.

Sidney stared at her, not sure whether he was still dreaming or was back on the bus. He found himself relaxing in the woman's presence. Her hand rested gently on his arm. It was reassuring.

"I'm Lilly Wood," the woman said. "That's my husband, Hiram." She pointed at the heavyset, jolly-looking man seated across the aisle, which was where Lilly had come from. He had a horseshoe of gray hair growing around the top of his head and a bushy salt-and-pepper beard. He looked like he could be related to Santa Claus.

"Hi there, young fella," Hiram said. "Didn't mean to interfere, but you were yelling pretty loud."

Sidney nodded. He was still getting his bearings.

"We got on in Roanoke," Lilly said. "I was watching you sleep. I hope you don't mind. It's been a long time since I watched a boy sleep."

"That's all right," Sidney said. He saw that Hiram was smiling at him, so he smiled back. "I'm sorry I bothered you."

"Nothing to be sorry about," Hiram said. "What's your name?"

"Larry Luckman," Sidney said.

"Well, that's a fine name," Hiram said. "Sounds lucky to me." He chuckled. "Doesn't it sound lucky to you, Lilly?"

"It certainly does," Lilly said. She never took her eyes off Sidney. "We were just going to have an early lunch. We'd be pleased if you joined us."

"I wouldn't mind," Sidney said. "Thank you." The dream, which he'd already forgotten, had left him hungry.

Hiram handed Lilly a shopping bag, from which she extracted a number of small boxes. "We're having fried chicken, mashed potatoes, coleslaw, and biscuits."

"I'm a vegetarian," Sidney said.

"Good for you," Lilly responded. "You can have

potatoes, coleslaw, and a biscuit. There's blueberry pie for dessert. Those little individual ones."

"I've been thinking about becoming a vegetarian myself," Hiram said, sinking his teeth into a chicken leg.

Lilly opened a box and took out the chicken, then handed the box to Sidney. "I bought two of these for Hiram, but he only needs one. There's lemonade to wash it down." She poured him a cup.

"Thank you," Sidney said, digging in.

"My pleasure," Lilly said. "He's a polite boy, isn't he?" She directed this remark to her husband.

"He's a dandy," Hiram said.

Lilly nibbled on a thigh and watched Sidney eat. "What's your destination, Lucky?" she asked. "You don't mind if I call you Lucky, do you? Because I think you are a very lucky boy."

"I don't mind," Sidney said. He liked the sound of it. And he figured he could use some luck right about now. "I'm on my way to New York City."

"Big place," Hiram said.

"Your folks meeting you there?" Lilly asked.

"My folks disappeared trying to cross the Pacific Ocean in a rowboat," Sidney said.

"That's a shame," Hiram said.

"An uncle or an aunt maybe," Lilly said.

"Nobody is meeting me," Sidney said. "I don't need anybody to meet me. I'm on my own. I'm older than I look. I've been around. I'm going to acting school. I'm going to be on the stage. Larry Luckman is going to be a star." He filled his mouth with coleslaw.

He's perfect, thought Lilly.

Hiram looked at Sidney with open approval.

"Acting can be a dicey line of work," Lilly said.

"Life is dicey," Sidney said.

"Doesn't he remind you of Gerald?" Hiram said.

Sidney didn't see how he could remind anybody of anybody.

"He does," Lilly said. "Not physically, of course. Gerald was larger and he had the one deformed arm. But the eyes are the same and they sound a lot alike. Don't they sound a lot alike, Hiram?"

"They do," Hiram said, working his way through a breast.

"We live on the way to Hummelstown," Lilly said. "Not far from Harrisburg."

"One of my ancestors acted with John Wilkes Booth," Sidney said. "He was on the stage with him the night President Lincoln was shot."

"That's very impressive," Hiram said.

"He gave up acting after that," Sidney said. "He never went in a theater again. But it's in my blood. I was destined to be an actor."

"We have a big house out there," Lilly said. "Too big for the two of us. There's a big empty bedroom upstairs with its own bathroom just going to waste."

"Gerald's old room," Hiram said.

"And there's a big porch on two sides with chairs and a swing. And a big yard."

"Don't forget the TV room," Hiram said.

"Hiram owns a hardware store," Lilly said.

"Not as exciting as acting, but a good solid business. Everybody needs hardware." He took a business card from his pocket and handed it to Sidney. "Hiram's Hardware," he said.

Sidney studied the card.

"Been in business thirty-six years," Hiram said. He looked sad.

"There's no one to leave it to," Lilly said. "Gerald was going to come into the business, but then he had the accident. He was fourteen. He got hit by a car getting off the school bus."

"Cars are supposed to stop for school buses," Hiram said.

"I saw it from the front door," Lilly said. "I was waiting for him there like I did every day."

"We don't want to get into all that," Hiram said, unwrapping his blueberry pie.

"No we don't," Lilly agreed.

Sidney didn't want to either. He felt bad for Gerald. Having a deformed arm couldn't have been easy. Getting hit by a car was worse.

"You got an acting school all picked out, Lucky?"

Hiram asked, eyeing his pie, then taking a large, satisfying bite out of it.

"I have several in mind," Sidney said. "I have to audition first. They don't take just anybody. Not the good ones. I'm going to make TV commercials to support myself. Back home I was in a lot of productions. I always got good reviews. At the orphanage they did a musical every year, and I was always the most important character." Sidney attacked his blueberry pie.

Lilly sighed. "There are so many children being abandoned these days," she said. "So many running away because they're not wanted or, even worse, abused." She clucked her tongue.

"It's terrible not having anybody," Hiram said. "I was an orphan myself. If I hadn't been taken in by a family who just up and offered, I don't know what would have happened to me."

"I know what you mean," Sidney said. His mouth was blue. He emptied his cup of lemonade. Lilly poured him more.

"Think we should?" Hiram asked.

"Worst thing he can do is say no," Lilly responded.

Sidney saw them both smiling at him. They were reaching out. They were drawing him in.

"This is going to sound strange," Lilly said, "and I know it's happening awful quick, but sometimes you have to take a chance that something's right. We'd like you to come live with us, Lucky. Get off with us in Harrisburg and come to Hummelstown and go to school and work a little at the hardware store and share our lives."

"If you don't like it," Hiram added quickly, "we'll bring you back to the bus station in Harrisburg and you can travel on to New York City. Anytime you want. No questions asked. No reasons required. We're just asking you to give it a try."

"We're looking for a son, Lucky," Lilly said, "and we think you might be looking for a family."

21

What If?

"Ten minutes to Harrisburg," the driver announced. "Ten minutes to the Harrisburg station."

Lilly and Hiram were looking at Sidney, their smiles still set in place, their expressions expectant. "You got any questions?" Hiram asked.

Sidney thought for a moment. "Can I fix up the bedroom? Hang pictures on the walls? Put in a big bookcase?"

"It's your room," Lilly said.

"I can change whatever I want?"

"Right down to the doorknobs," Hiram said.

"And I can be a vegetarian?"

"You can eat whatever makes you happy," Lilly said. "I'll cook all your favorite foods."

"What about my head?"

"What about it?" Lilly asked.

"You don't mind it being so big?"

"Just more of you to admire," Lilly said.

"All I can see is you need a larger hat size," Hiram said.

"I don't want to go to school," Sidney said. "I don't like school."

"I don't think that's a problem," Lilly said. "Do you think it's a problem, Hiram?"

"No, I don't, Lilly. We'll say he's our nephew who's visiting." He looked past Lilly to Sidney. "If you decide to stay, I'll get some papers that say you're sixteen. You can get papers for anything these days."

"Harrisburg," the driver announced. "We'll be stopping in Harrisburg for fifteen minutes. Don't forget your personal belongings. If you're traveling on, keep an eye on the time."

"And I can leave if I don't like it?"

"Pack your bag and you're on your way," Hiram said.

Who could ask for a better offer than this? What did he have to lose? He liked these people. They wanted him. They were the grandparents he'd never had. It was like he'd ordered them from a catalog. It was certainly better than not knowing what was going to happen to him when he got to New York City. If he liked Hummelstown, he'd stay. If he didn't, he'd head out.

"Okay," Sidney said. "I'll do it."

For a moment Lilly and Hiram seemed stunned by Sidney's decision, then they beamed their happiness. Lilly threw her arms around him.

"Why, that's the best news I've heard in a long time," Hiram said. "I knew there was something special about you, Lucky. A kindred spirit."

They got off the bus like they'd been a family their whole lives. Lilly and Hiram got their things from the baggage compartment, then they went together into the waiting room. Sidney took a look back at the bus. He could change his mind whenever he wanted to. He could turn around right now and get back on it if he wanted to.

"The truck is parked in a lot," Hiram said to Sidney. "It's only a short walk."

"I have to go to the bathroom," Sidney said.

"We can stop on the road," Lilly said.

"I have to go now."

"If you can hold it awhile, we'll stop for the best homemade ice cream you ever tasted," Lilly said.

"I can't hold it," Sidney said. "I have to go to the bathroom now."

"Let him go," Hiram said, giving Sidney a pat on the back. "You go ahead, Lucky."

"I'll hold your bag," Lilly said, reaching to pull it from Sidney's shoulder.

"My bag goes with me," Sidney said, pulling away. "My bag goes everywhere I go."

"You don't need your bag to go to the bathroom," Lilly said, an edge of impatience creeping into her voice.

"Let him take his bag," Hiram said, sounding jovial. "A man doesn't like being separated from his personal belongings." He winked at Sidney. "We'll be right here."

Lilly and Hiram watched Sidney make his way to the men's room. "We're going to have to keep an eye on him," Lilly said.

"Don't be so jumpy," Hiram said. "Everything will be all right. I'll go get the truck. You guard the door."

"I won't take the chance that somebody will take him away from me."

"Nobody's taking him away, Lilly," Hiram said. Lilly moved closer to the men's room door. She wasn't letting this one escape.

A man left as Sidney walked in. Another left as he stepped to the urinal. He was alone. He had trouble relieving himself. He felt all knotted up inside. Something was happening. Something he didn't understand. He tried to analyze it. Was it Lilly and Hiram? He didn't think so. He didn't really know them very well, but they didn't seem to be the problem. He had nothing to go back to and nothing to look forward to up ahead, so that wasn't it. What was nagging him? Why was he starting to have an anxiety attack? Maybe it was the way Lilly had grabbed at his bag. That couldn't be it. She was just trying to help. He looked over at the door and knew suddenly that he couldn't go back through it. He heard Moses Longfellow speaking to him. He had to make this journey alone or he wouldn't get to its end. That was what was wrong. It wasn't over yet. He had to keep going.

He looked around and spotted the window high up on the wall. It was open, but there was no way he could reach it. There was nothing to climb on. Somehow he had to get himself and his bag up there and out, and he didn't have much time. He thought Hiram might appear at any moment to find out what was taking him so long. A toilet flushed and a stall door opened, startling Sidney. Out stepped the biggest kid he'd ever seen. He must have been six foot five and two hundred and fifty pounds. He couldn't have been more than sixteen or seventeen years old.

"Hey, Melonhead," the kid said, moving to the sink to wash his hands. "How you doing?"

"I'm doing good," Sidney said. He'd let the reference to his head pass. He needed this kid to help him. But how? If he just asked outright and the kid said no, he was sunk. But why would the kid say no? All he wanted to do was get out the window. "How you doing?" he asked.

"I'm going to college on a scholarship to play football," the kid said. "That's how I'm doing. Then I'm going to be a pro. That's how I'm doing. Then I'm going to make big money. That's how I'm doing."

"Me too," Sidney said.

The kid looked at him like he was crazy, then burst out laughing. "You're okay," the kid said.

Sidney grinned. "So are you," he said. "Could I have your autograph?" Maybe that would oil the machine a little.

"Sure," the kid said, pleased.

Sidney fished around in his duffel bag and came out with his notebook and one of his ballpoint pens. He glanced at the door. He had to hurry. "Make it to Banjo Peabody," he said. "That's me."

"Banjo Peabody it is," the kid said. "I'm Bigboy Ball. I was born big and I'm still growing. You'll be hearing about me." He wrote out a message, a slow letter at a time, then signed it with a practiced flourish and handed the notebook back to Sidney. "It says, To my pal Banjo Peabody. It was good meeting you. Signed, Bigboy Ball."

"Thanks," Sidney said. He admired what Bigboy had written for an appropriate moment, then stuffed the notebook and pen back into his duffel bag and zipped it shut. He glanced at the door again. He looked up at his new friend. "Bigboy, I was wondering if you could help me out with something."

Just outside the door, Lilly paced back and forth, her irritation growing by the second. What was he doing in there? Another minute and I'm going in, she thought, I don't care if it is the men's room.

"Take care of yourself, Banjo," Bigboy Ball said as he lifted Sidney and his bag to the window. "I won't say anything to those people waiting out there."

"I appreciate it, Bigboy," Sidney said, pushing his bag out. "Good luck." He worked his way through the window, then dropped to the ground and started running for the bus. As it pulled away he saw Lilly and Hiram looking for him. Maybe they'd find another boy, but something in him hoped not.

22

The Big Apple

Through the purple haze of late afternoon, Sidney got his first look at the Manhattan skyline. Its jagged peaks rose above each other like a range of man-made mountains that were every bit as awe-inspiring as the Olympics or Cascades. From the window of the bus the city seemed wondrous and mysterious. His excitement grew. Was this to be his journey's end? Would he find his new life here? He swallowed hard and felt the sourness of uncertainty churning in his stomach. He'd have to leave the bus and face the unknown to find out. The world went dark. They were in a tunnel beneath the Hudson River.

When he stepped out of the bus station onto

Eighth Avenue, the heat smacked him in the face. The temperature was ninety-two degrees and holding. The humidity was a fat ninety percent. His face beaded with sweat. His shirt turned damp and stuck to his skin. Spread out in front of him were more people than he'd ever seen in one place in his life. Despite the heat they were moving with energy and purpose. The noise, the aggregate sound produced by this mass of humanity and the endless stream of cars and trucks and buses and the constant racket of horns and jackhammers and sirens, was overwhelming. Sidney smiled to himself. He was here. He'd made it. He wanted to explore the city's streets, to see everything there was to see, but he didn't have the slightest idea which way to go or what to look at first.

He studied the panorama in front of him, looking for some sign that would help him decide where to begin. But there was nothing that helped. So he just started walking, his duffel bag strap held with a tight grip. He walked slowly, as though he didn't have a care in the world, like a tourist trying to take in everything at once. He saw street vendors hawking watches and straw hats and bottled water and fans and boom boxes and jewelry. He heard half a dozen languages being spoken. He smelled the exotic perfume of foods from a dozen countries being cooked in tiny restaurants. He was bumped into and jostled as the stream of people passed around him. "Excuse me," they said. "Sorry," they said. He wondered how so many people could be so crammed together and still get along with each other. He heard somebody yelling behind him.

"Hey, you, kid, out of my way!"

He stepped aside to make room for a woman of indeterminate age, who was dressed in layer upon layer of ragged clothing. She was pushing a shopping cart filled with plastic garbage bags that bulged with what Sidney took to be her worldly possessions.

"It's hot," she yelled as she passed him.

"Yes it is," he yelled back.

She hurried on and turned a corner into an alley and was gone. She hadn't even looked at him.

He changed directions and saw that the street numbers were getting higher. He was on Sixth Avenue, in a canyon of office buildings. The hustle and bustle was even more intense here. More people. More traffic. More noise. At the corner of Fifty-second Street he stopped to listen to a man reciting poetry above the din. He came to the end of Sixth Avenue and saw a park across the street. He dodged traffic and entered it and felt in an instant that he'd made his way into the countryside. It was filled with trees and paths and meadows. It was quiet here. Peaceful. He came to a wading pool, which was filled with laughing, splashing children. He yearned to be in the water with them. He moved on to a bridge, where he stood and watched rowers on a lake. He heard the clip-clop of a horse and turned and saw it pulling an open carriage with a man and woman and two small children in it. He came to a zoo, where he visited with the monkeys for a while. Monkeys always cheered him up.

He left Central Park and saw a great plaza with a fountain at its middle. There were more horse-drawn carriages here. There were hot-dog carts and pretzel stands and cart after cart offering cold drinks: orange juice and apple juice and lemonade and mango juice and papaya juice and guava juice. He studied the people he passed more closely now. Mostly they ignored him. Mostly they ignored each other. But every once in a while somebody hurled out a "How you doing?" or a "What's up?" or threw out a smile. He marveled at how they gave each other room to move about without ever slowing down. He saw them open doors for each other. He heard a taxi driver yelling at a cop, who paid no attention. He watched a man coming toward him yelling obscenities as though he had no control over what he was saying. Nobody seemed to mind.

He crossed the street right in the middle, like everybody else. In Seattle and Los Angeles you could get a ticket for jaywalking. Here it was hard to cross the street if you didn't jaywalk. Sidney figured that the whole of downtown Seattle would disappear in Manhattan. Compared with this, Los Angeles was as flat as a pancake.

He heard the rumble of noise beneath his feet and looked down. He was standing on a grate. A subway train was passing below. Hot air shot up his pant legs. He found the entrance to a station, made his way down the stairs, paid his fare, and got on the first train that came along. He didn't care where it was going. He'd ride for a while, then get off and start walking again. He'd never ridden underground before. The speed of the train exhilarated him. A blind man with a Seeing Eye dog walked through his subway car playing an accordion and singing opera. Sidney fished in his pocket and put all his change in the cup fastened to the accordion. The man said thankyou. Around him people read newspapers and books or slept or stared off into space or talked above the clatter.

Four stops later, Sidney returned to the street. He walked west until he saw the Empire State Building, which he recognized right away from the movie *King Kong*. The original black-and-white version, which was one of Sid's favorites. And his. He rode the elevator to the observation deck. He looked out over the island of Manhattan. He could see Queens and Long Island and Staten Island and New Jersey and Brooklyn. He looked for a long time at Central Park, trying to pick out the places he'd been. He watched the ships in the harbor. He studied the Statue of Liberty. He counted the bridges that crossed the East River and the Hudson. He watched a ship heading out toward the Atlantic Ocean and wondered where it was going and what it would be like to be going with it.

What he couldn't see from where he was standing was how he could fit in here. It was all well and good that nobody seemed to notice his head, but nobody noticed him at all. They were all too busy, too intent on what they were doing and where they were going. It was too big, this city, too much for somebody who was twelve years old and on his own. Seeing it all laid out before him, Sidney understood that this wasn't the end of his journey. He had someplace else to go. He had no idea where. He thought about King Kong clinging to the side of this building, hanging on for dear life. He thought that all the great ape wanted was a little understanding.

23

Day to Night

He took the elevator back down to the street and started walking again. The city was changing. The people who worked in it and lived somewhere else were on their way home. There weren't so many cars now. Not so many trucks. Not so much horn honking. The jackhammers had gone silent. The air seemed softer somehow in the dusk. People weren't walking so fast. They seemed more relaxed, as though, having survived the day, they could afford to let their guard down. The city seemed more human to Sidney, more like a bunch of small towns all connected together than the metropolis that had greeted him a few hours earlier. He looked for a place to eat. He was ravenous. He didn't want to spend much money. Since he had no idea where he was going next, he had no idea how much it would cost him to get there. He passed a hole-in-the-wall coffee shop that looked like it would fit the bill.

It was cold inside. The air conditioner rattled and creaked and dripped water on the floor.

"Sit anywhere," the waitress said. "Be right with you." She had an accent that made it sound like she was talking through her nose.

The cook, who was turning bacon on the grill, gave him a three-second once-over, then went back to work.

Sidney sat at the far end of the short counter and swung around on his stool to inspect the place. A man and woman sat at the other end of the counter, which was covered with worn industrial gray Formica. A man sat alone at one of the three tables that lined the wall. The coffee shop was so small that if you sat at a table you could just stand and take your food from the waitress as she leaned over the counter to pass it to you. Which was what she did as Sidney watched. A club sandwich with a side of fries. The eight stools that lined the counter had more tape on them than fabric. They squealed like little pigs when you turned on them. The cook was bald except for two tufts of black hair that grew above his ears. Sidney turned and saw that the waitress was standing in front of him. She was a stick of a woman.

"Let me know when you're ready," she said, setting a glass of water and a menu in front of him.

Sidney emptied the glass of water in two gulps and set it down, and a minute later the waitress refilled it. He drank that glass just as quickly.

"Gotta stay hydrated," she said, filling it a third time.

Sidney studied the menu. "I'll have a grilled cheese sandwich and potato salad," he said when the waitress passed by. "And more water, please."

"Plenty of water," she said. "All you can drink."

He looked up at the clock. It was nearly eight. Which made it nearly five in Seattle and Los Angeles. Sid was probably still at work. His mother would be cooking dinner for Devers and his stepbrother, William, who could do no wrong. School would start soon. In a couple of weeks. But not for Sidney. He didn't have a school to go to.

"Pick up!" the cook yelled, even though the waitress was standing only a few feet away.

She set Sidney's food in front of him. "Extra pickles," she said, putting the dish next to his potato salad. "More where they came from."

He ate slowly. What was the hurry? He had no place to go tonight. He had nothing to do except find somewhere to sleep. A hotel was out of the question. It didn't matter how cheap it was, it would be too much.

"Too hot this summer," the man down the counter from Sidney said to him.

"Too hot," Sidney echoed.

"You got that right," the man said. He paid his bill. "Take it easy," he said to the cook and the waitress.

"Take it easy," the cook yelled back.

"See you tomorrow," the waitress said.

The man and the woman he was with got to their feet. "Stay out of trouble," the man said to Sidney. "If you can't, don't get caught."

"I'll do my best," Sidney said. He watched them leave. It wasn't any different here than riding on the bus, he thought. People came and people went. Nothing was permanent. He was tired of that. Tired of moving. He'd spent his whole life since he was six bouncing back and forth. He wanted to unpack his bag and leave it unpacked. He wanted to wake up every morning in the same place. A place that he wasn't afraid of. A place that was normal, whatever normal was.

"How about some dessert?" the waitress asked.

"No thank you," Sidney said, trying not to look at the pies on the shelf behind the counter.

"We close in an hour," she said. "I've got only two slices of cherry left. It's on the house." She brought him the largest piece and poured him a glass of milk. "You can't eat cherry pie with water," she said.

When he'd picked the last crumb of piecrust off the plate and finished his milk, he went to the bathroom. There was a blackboard on one wall that contained telephone numbers and messages, mostly from people who wanted other people to call them or who had things to trade or sell. Sidney tried to think of something to write, then picked up the piece of chalk. In small letters he printed "This is an excellent place to eat." He used the toilet, then washed his hands and face. He brushed his teeth because he wasn't sure when he'd get the chance again.

He returned to the counter and paid and thanked the waitress and left her a dollar. He heard Mona Lipp's voice in his ear. He stepped back out onto the sidewalk. It was still hot enough to wilt a flower.

And Then to Sleep

It was nearly dark as Sidney set out to see more of the city. He walked uptown again and found himself in a district of theaters and restaurants and bars. The sidewalks were filled with people who seemed to glow with merriment. Limousines discharged well-dressed passengers who moved with the grace and confidence of royalty. Everybody seemed headed for a big party.

Ahead he saw what looked like an eruption of light. It was Times Square, which wasn't a square at all but a crossroads where Forty-second Street and Seventh Avenue and Broadway all intersected. He stopped at the edge of it to take in the light show:

the pulsating neon and flashing lightbulbs and giant video screens that advertised soft drinks and airlines and places to eat and banks and cameras and Broadway plays and movies and music. It was an electronic wonderland.

He headed downtown and walked through a neighborhood of brownstones and small apartment houses. He heard the murmur of conversation. He saw people sitting on their front stoops, dressed in shorts and undershirts, sipping iced drinks and fanning themselves. He watched a group of little kids playing hide-and-seek. He heard their parents calling out to them to stay close.

He walked on, heading west toward the Hudson River, moving into a neighborhood of run-down buildings and storefront businesses whose windows and doors were covered with iron bars. He encountered fewer and fewer people as he made his way across Eighth Avenue and headed for Ninth, then Tenth. He was looking for a place to sleep now, where nobody would bother him, especially the police. How could he explain himself if he was caught? A boy on the streets all by himself this late at night? They'd find out who he was and send him back.

He passed a group of homeless men who wanted money. He kept moving. He had nothing to give. Once he had to run when an aggressive drunk wanted his duffel bag and came after him. He kept searching for some small corner of the city where he could close his eyes without worry.

He thought he heard footsteps behind him. He looked back, but no one was there. Maybe all he was hearing was the thumping of his heart. His mouth was dry. The duffel bag's strap dug into his shoulder. He shifted it to the other side. He picked up his pace. He glanced quickly across the street and saw the dim outline of three people keeping pace with him. He didn't see the other two who came up behind him and grabbed his arms.

Sidney cried out in alarm, but no sound came from his throat. He saw the three forms across the street moving toward him. He struggled to be free, trying to flail his arms and twist his shoulders, but there was no escape. He felt fingers digging into his arms.

"Let him go." It was a command from the leader of the pack, a kid not much older than Sidney. He wasn't the largest of them, but he was clearly the toughest. The kids holding him stepped back. The leader approached Sidney and looked him in the eye, like an animal taking the measure of his prey. Sidney looked at the other four kids. They varied in age and size, but none seemed older than thirteen or fourteen. They all wore baggy pants that hung low on their hips and loose T-shirts and high-tops. It was hard to see their faces clearly in the dark.

One of the kids pushed Sidney, and he stumbled

forward, then caught himself. He wobbled, light-headed from fear. He took a deep breath and found the calm and determination to try to talk his way out of this. When he looked up he saw that he was in the middle of a circle, the hub of a wheel.

"I'm lost," Sidney managed. "I've got to get to the bus station or I'll miss my bus. It's the last one tonight. I'm going to Boston." Boston? Where had Boston come from? "Anytime you come to Boston, I'll show you around." The Red Sox were in Boston. Paul Revere had ridden his horse in Boston. That was what he knew about Boston.

"He don't sound like he's from Boston," one of the kids said.

"He's got a head like he's from Boston," another kid said. "Like a giant bean."

"He's got some nut on him," the last kid said.

"Looks like a melon."

"Melonhead."

They all said it after that. One after the other. "Melonhead." "Melonhead." "Melonhead." "Melon-head." "Melonhead." It sounded like cannon fire.

A car drove by, bathing them in white light. Sidney waved at it, hoping it would stop, hoping that the people in it would help him. The car drove on.

"If you can get out of the circle," the leader said, "we'll take you to the bus station."

Sidney looked at him and tried to smile. "I'm just trying to get somewhere," he said.

"We're all trying to get somewhere," the leader said. He smiled back.

"Let's get this over with," one of the kids said.

"Come on, Melonhead, give it a try," the leader said. "It's the only chance you have." He sounded amused.

Sidney chose the two smallest kids in the circle. The gap between them was maybe four feet wide. He looked away from them and locked on to two others. Deception was everything. Deception was all he had. And maybe the element of surprise. If he did it right.

"When should I go?" he asked, turning to the leader. He charged without waiting for an answer. He put his head down and made for one of the kids he'd picked. He ran as hard as he could. He saw the kid pull his fist back to hit him. He feinted in one direction, then another, then did a one-hundred-and-eighty-degree spin. The punch missed him by a foot. He spun back in the other direction to distract the second kid, then spun a third time and found nobody in front of him and lunged to be free from the circle. He cried out as he was hit and fell to the ground, twisting his ankle, inches short of his goal. The circle closed in around him.

They hit him and never said a word. He punched out wildly and occasionally found a target. He felt blood running from his nose. When he quit fighting back, one of them kicked him. He moaned.

"Grab the bag," the leader said.

"Don't take my bag," Sidney tried to say. His voice sounded far away.

"I went easy on you because of your head," the leader said. He squatted down next to Sidney. "You'll be okay," he said. "You'll make it." He rifled through Sidney's pockets and took his wallet and money. "Take care of yourself, Melonhead." He patted Sidney on the shoulder and stood. "To get to the bus station, you go back the way you came. Three blocks. You go left and walk until you come to it. Watch out for the transit cops. They don't like kids."

Sidney heard them fighting over his bag as they left. He waited until they were gone, then tried to move. He couldn't believe how much he hurt. It was like a bad dream. He tried to stand but couldn't. He rolled to his side, then onto his stomach. He rested in that position, then pushed himself up so that he was on his hands and knees. He rested again, then steeled himself and crawled to the doorway of an abandoned storefront. He spent the night there, huddled in the dark, his eyes wide open.

25

The Last Leg

The morning was bright with promise. The air was fresh. The temperature was in the seventies. Everything seemed crisp and new.

The bus headed east on Interstate 95. Sidney stared dully out the window at Connecticut. His body pulsated with pain. He was beginning to get used to it. He shifted in his seat, looking for comfort, and winced. He started drifting off to sleep and pulled himself back. He sat up as straight as he could and winced again.

Only a few hours had passed since he'd forced himself to his feet in the storefront doorway. The sky had been blue-black in the east. New York City was coming to life. It was time to move on. He'd brushed himself off, then struggled out of his T-shirt, turned it inside out, and struggled back into it. Five minutes had been required to complete that simple task. Raising his hands above his head was sheer torture. His legs had felt like water-soaked logs. He'd barely been able to put one foot in front of the other. He'd walked as quickly as he could, driven by his obsession to continue his journey. He'd put the full power of his will into walking like a normal person.

He'd stopped by a door just inside the bus station to look for cops. He didn't see any. What chance did he have to get away in his condition if he did? He'd made his way to the men's room. It hurt to pee. It hurt to wash his face and hands. He couldn't pick at the caked blood beneath his nose because it would start bleeding again. There was a purplish swelling under his right eye, and his left cheek was puffy and tender. He was bruised everywhere, but most of it didn't show. He'd reached down into the back of his underwear and removed the fifty dollars he'd hidden there after Shamus Flowers picked his pocket. He'd taken a last look at himself in the mirror and worked some water into his hair, so it looked like he'd just taken a shower. He'd stood as tall and as straight as he could, and he'd gone to buy his ticket for the first bus to Boston. He hadn't cared that it was a local. He'd just wanted to get started.

———————

Sidney opened his eyes. He'd been sleeping despite himself. He was still in Connecticut. It was hours yet to Boston. He didn't know how long it would take to get from there to the tip of Cape Cod. This was his destination now. Provincetown. He'd seen it on the map at the bus station. It looked to him like the end of the country.

He thought about the kids who'd beaten and robbed him. He knew he should be angry, but he wasn't. Not anymore. They were like a pack of wild dogs. That was their life. They did what they had to to survive. He remembered the leader squatting to talk to him and seeing, in that otherwise inscrutable face, a flash of bewilderment and uncertainty every bit as profound as his own.

He lost his battle with sleep again, free-falling into a black hole of lost time. In what seemed only a few moments, a voice pulled him back to consciousness.

"This is Middleport," the driver announced. "We'll be stopping here for three minutes. Middleport, Rhode Island."

Sidney peered out the window at the main business street of the village. It was crowded this early afternoon in August. The tourists were out in all their splendor, shopping at the many shops, walking the narrow streets that were lined with houses mostly built in the seventeen hundreds. They stood on docks and photographed the fishing boats and pleasure craft. They photographed everything. Middleport was picture-perfect photogenic. A tiny Venice set on Narragansett Bay.

He couldn't believe he was here. He'd never thought about where the bus might stop on its way to Boston. He turned away from the window. He didn't want to see this place. He didn't want to think about it. He was going to Provincetown. The engine started. The door closed. The brakes released. Sidney jumped to his feet. "Stop," he yelled. "I have to get off."

26

An Unscheduled Stop

He watched the bus pull away, immediately sorry that he'd gotten off. What was wrong with him? He didn't want to be here. His response to hearing the name of the place, to seeing the street, to realizing suddenly where he was, had taken him so completely by surprise that he'd acted like an idiot. It was a mistake. He'd stay right where he was and wait for the next bus. Maybe he'd hitchhike. He looked around to get his bearings. He recognized Sawyer's Market. He'd gone shopping with her there. This was where his grandmother Alice lived. This was where he'd come as a child to see her. He didn't like Alice. She didn't like him. She was a reason to stay on the bus, not a reason to get off. He saw that he was being looked at by everyone who passed. He heard whispers. A man and woman waiting to cross the street were gawking at him. Somebody took his picture.

"I can't help it," he shouted. "My head is big because I have Helium's disease. Every day my head gets bigger. Someday it's going to get so big that it'll lift me off the ground and I'll float up into the sky and disappear forever." Helium's disease. That was a good one. He almost laughed.

There was an opening in the stream of traffic, and he moved as quickly as he could between two cars, then walked stiff-legged into the drugstore, which was where, according to the sign in the window, you bought bus tickets. The lady at the cash register told him that the next bus to Boston was in four hours. He bought a Milky Way.

He wandered up one side of the main business street and down the other, peering into store windows, trying to work out the cramps that had accumulated from sitting so long on the bus. The pain from the beating had turned into a constant dull ache. He reached the village green. It occupied one side of Middleport's busiest intersection, a triangular conjunction of its three main streets. The World War One Memorial was here. The bookstore, the weekly newspaper office, a bank, an insurance office, an antiques store, the barbershop, and a store filled with locally produced doodads lined the other two sides.

Sidney turned on his axis, a slow circle, trying to decide which way to go. He wasn't going to walk back and forth on the same street for four hours. That left West Carpenter Street, which led out of town in the direction of Providence and Boston, and Carpenter Street, which led to the town dock.

He walked slowly, keeping his head down lest his grandmother drive by and see him or, worse, encounter him on foot. Despite her having seen him only a couple of times when he was a child, he knew she'd recognize him in an instant. For the same reason that he'd make a lousy bank robber. Once seen, his visage was forever imprinted upon the memory. He told himself to stop acting crazy. He walked faster. He'd hold his head up and take his chances.

At the dock he asked a man who looked like Ichabod Crane what time it was, then let the man record him for posterity with his new digital camera. He had three and a half hours to kill before the bus showed up. He walked along the edge of the dock, past the empty berths of fishing boats that were out for the day. He stopped by a piling and leaned against it and looked out over the harbor and the bay, which was beyond the breakwater. He heard a small child's laughter and turned to see a boy in a stroller amusing himself with his fingers, as though they were the greatest discovery ever made. Silently he wished the boy a better future than the one he saw for himself.

He looked back toward the bay. The air smelled of salt water and mud. It was low tide. A small squadron of seagulls lazed about above the channel looking for afternoon treats. A speedboat filled with teenagers passed slowly through the channel. The boat was straining like a large dog pulling against its leash, and Sidney could tell that the blond boy at the wheel was dying to gun it. Who cared about the seven-knot speed limit? Water skis hung out over the stern. He watched the girls in their bathing suits, their lithe bodies tanned to a golden brown, and felt a yearning. It was like the low growl of summer thunder heard in the far distance.

He left the dock and started walking the side streets and lanes of the village. He paid no attention to his direction, gave no conscious thought to a destination. His mind was focused on the waning day. What if he didn't get to Boston in time for the last bus to Provincetown? What if he had to spend the night in Boston? On the streets? He wouldn't do that again. He'd rather spend the night here, in some out-of-the-way spot where no one would bother him. In the bushes if he had to. It was warm enough. He had some money for food, a little. He could get the bus in the morning. What difference would a day make?

When he glanced up to see where he was, he found himself looking at his grandmother's house. It was bold yellow, with dark green and white trim. It was big. There were six apartments inside. Two down and two up in front and two in back. Alice lived in the larger of the two downstairs fronts, which was the largest apartment in the building. She rented the others.

The sound of Sidney's heart thumping resonated inside his head. What was he supposed to do about this? Why was he here? He had to consider the possibility that seeing his grandmother was part of his quest. Maybe he'd been coming here all along. This could be the end of his journey, or it could be like all the other places he'd been since leaving Los Angeles, just another stop along the way. He didn't know if he could trust his grandmother. He had no idea how she'd react when she saw him or what she'd say. He didn't want to think about the consequences of his decision. He wouldn't be here if he wasn't supposed to be. He had to go by that. That was all there was.

He crossed the street and went up the half dozen steps on the west side of the house. He smelled the sweet fragrance of the honeysuckle that grew along the fence. He climbed the two steps to the landing, faced the door, and rang the bell.

27

The Initial Encounter

"What are you doing here?" Those were Alice's first words upon seeing Sidney. Then she looked past him, her eyes searching, her expression set with disbelief.

"Where's your mother?" she said next, her voice cross, sounding like she was ready for a battle.

Sidney looked up at his grandmother, a sixty-year-old woman with a handsome face and dyed bright red hair. She was wearing paint-smeared jeans and a T-shirt that looked like a much-used artist's palette.

"Seattle," he said, his voice climbing an octave.

"Don't tell me your father brought you. The man can't stand me."

"He's in Los Angeles."

She turned a hard eye on him.

"I'm alone," he said.

"What?"

"Alone. By myself. Just me."

"That's impossible. How did you get here? Never mind that now. Why are you here? How old are you? You're too young to travel by yourself. Does your mother know you're here?"

"I'm on my way to Boston," Sidney said, wishing more than ever that he'd stayed on the bus. "I'm going to a week of summer school at Harvard. It's for kids. A special program. I won an essay contest about life in other parts of the universe. I thought I'd stop on the way and say hello. It was good to see you."

He turned on his heel and started away. She had the door half closed before something compelled her to open it again. He wasn't more than twelve or thirteen. She couldn't remember. What was Meredith thinking, sending him across the country on his own?

"Come back here," she commanded.

He turned to face her. He stayed where he was. "I only have a couple of hours before the bus leaves," he said. Why don't I just keep walking, he wondered.

She eyed him skeptically, this ragtag boy with his hands thrust into his pockets, a defiant expression burnished onto his large, round, unhappy face.

"What happened to you?" she asked.

"Nothing happened to me," he said.

"The bruises. The blood under your nose."

"Street hockey," he said.

"Where's your stuff?"

"I left it with the lady at the drugstore. She said she'd make sure it was okay. I didn't want to lug it around with me." Why was he explaining himself to her? She didn't have anything to do with him.

She looked at him for another moment, then drew back and disappeared into her apartment, leaving the door open. "If you're coming in, come in," she said from the hall.

He entered warily. The first room off the hall was Alice's studio. It smelled of turpentine and paint. It must have been the parlor once upon a time. He found Alice standing in front of a large easel, which occupied the center of the room, staring at a canvas that measured five feet by five feet. She took no notice of him at all. He waited uneasily for her to say something. When she didn't, he moved carefully along the wall, which was lined with unframed paintings, until he could see what she was studying with such interest. It was a painting of vibrant colors and staccato shapes that seemed to Sidney to be the result of an explosion.

She darted forward suddenly, a three-inch house-painting brush in her hand, and created a new shape in cobalt blue. "You should do something to counteract the effect of your personal appearance," she said, stepping back to inspect what she'd just done. "You should do something about the way you dress."

"There's nothing so hot about the way you look," Sidney countered.

She looked over at him. "I was making an observation. Constructive criticism."

"I'm just making an observation, too," Sidney said. "You look like a witch."

"Maybe I am a witch," she said. "Maybe I'll make you disappear."

"Maybe I'd like you to make me disappear."

"Tall men do better in the world than short ones. Slim men do better than fat ones. Good-looking men do better than ugly ones. I didn't make that up. That's how it is. Those are the rules. You need something to set you apart. Do you have a discernible talent? Can you play the piano? Can you sing?"

"I can't do anything," he said, wishing he could, wishing he was all those things, tall and slim and good-looking.

"Well, you were smart enough to win an essay contest. Maybe you're a writer."

"I don't like writing. It's too much work."

"What do you like?"

"Nothing."

"You must be good at something."

"Nothing I can think of."

"You're interested in life on other planets. Maybe you could be a scientist. An astronomer maybe. A physicist. An astronaut. It doesn't matter what you look like to be any of those things."

"Yeah, right, with a head like mine I can see myself floating around in space. Maybe I wouldn't need one of those suits. Maybe the alien race that left me here by mistake would come back and get me."

"I'm not talking about your head. I'm talking about you. The whole package. Sidney T. Mellon, Junior. Your parents didn't do you any favors with that name. I don't know what they were thinking. I don't know what you were thinking when you stopped here."

"I don't know either."

"Obviously you don't like me."

"Obviously you don't like *me*."

"That's something we have in common," she said.

"I should have stayed on the bus," he said.

"I agree."

He started for the door.

She turned her attention back to the painting, trying to block him from her mind. She didn't like children. Not this close. They interfered and interrupted and generally caused trouble. Her life was in order. Sidney was disorder.

"How's your mother?" she said, casting a glance in his direction.

He backtracked a few steps, until he could see the painting again, before answering. None of his movements was hurried. "She's doing okay," he said.

"Still married to that creep?"

"He's a reptile," Sidney said. He hoped he wasn't giving snakes a bad name.

She added a streak of cobalt blue to another part of the painting. "And Sid's still Sid?"

"Sid's still Sid," he said.

She picked up another brush and worked yellow into it.

"What are you painting?"

"A picture."

"Of what?"

"Nothing."

"What's it about?"

"It isn't about anything."

"It must mean something."

"Whatever it means to you."

"You can't recognize anything in it."

"There's nothing to recognize. It's abstract. I'm what you call an abstract expressionist. I'm just not a very good one." She smiled. It softened her features. "You take what you have the way it comes and make the most of it."

He moved to get a better view of the painting. "Then why bother to do it?" he asked. "If you're not any good, what's the point?"

"I didn't say I'm not any good. I said I'm not very good. There's a difference. And the point is that it's how I express myself. Everybody should have a way of doing that. It makes me feel like I'm accomplishing something. Don't you have any attributes at all?"

"I can belch whenever I feel like it. Really loud when I want to."

"Then your future is assured." She laid down a slash of yellow.

"Is it okay to use the bathroom?"

"Through that door and to the left. Just keep going till you get there."

When he was gone, she put down her brush, angry at herself for reacting so strongly to his presence. He was just a kid. What was the big deal? She remembered him as a small child. She'd tried to be nice to him then. He'd been unruly and poked into everything and had asked a million questions. He'd brought dirt into her apartment. He'd been the source of friction. Meredith and Sid had fought long and loud on their last visit and had left Sidney in her care for a time. She hadn't enjoyed it one bit. She looked at her watch. He'll be leaving soon, she thought. I can deal with him until then. And she had tonight to look forward to. She shook her head in wonder. How had her overprotective daughter ever allowed her precious son to travel three thousand miles by himself? Maybe Meredith had changed.

Sidney studied his reflection in the mirror above the sink. He had to stand on his toes to see himself. He saw clearly what he was and always would be. There was no avoiding it. He was aware of how banged up he was and how bad he smelled. He wanted to take a shower and put on clean clothes. He was so tired he thought he'd fall asleep on his feet.

Alice was still in front of the painting when he returned. She'd decided in his absence that it wasn't working.

"I was wondering if you had anything to eat," Sidney said as he moved back into the room. His stomach growled as if on cue.

"Aren't you going to miss your bus?"

"I have time to eat."

"I'm not sure what I have."

"I'll go wait at the drugstore," he said. "Thanks for everything." He started for the door, then stopped. He didn't want to leave. He wanted to sleep in a bed. He didn't want to spend the night afraid.

"I don't really have to be there until tomorrow," he said. "There's a bus in the morning."

"Are you asking to spend the night?" She looked at him with a critical eye.

"I thought you might invite me," he said. "You are

my grandmother. I thought it might be a good opportunity."

"For what?"

"For . . . forget about it."

"I have plans tonight," she said. "If you'd given me some notice, I could have canceled."

"Sure. Fine. No problem. Next time I'll call you from the bus on my cell phone. I thought you might be interested in spending some time with me. I don't know when I'll be back again. I'm sorry I bothered."

He took another couple of steps toward the door, then stopped and looked back. One more try. "I'm a day early," he said. "I can't move into the dorm until tomorrow." He couldn't read her reaction. He was running out of reasons.

"Your mother must have made some arrangement."

"She got mixed up and sent me a day too soon," he said, taking another step toward the door. "I'll stay at a hotel."

"Do you have any idea how expensive a hotel room in Boston is?" she said.

"What choice do I have?"

"Do you have enough money?"

He shrugged off the question.

"How much do you have?"

"What do you care where I stay or what I have? You're not interested in me. You're only interested in yourself."

"Don't get smart with me, Sidney. I'm not your mother."

"You're not even my grandmother," he said, heading for the door, this time intent on making it.

She bit her bottom lip and said exactly what she didn't want to say. She told him to go get his bags.

He was momentarily discombobulated. First, because she'd said he could spend the night. Second, because he had no bags. He'd completely forgotten. Now he'd have to make up another story. "I'll go right now," he said. He'd think of something. "I'll be right back."

"Are they heavy? I can get my car."

"No. There's only one. Just enough stuff for a week. It's not heavy. I can do it myself. I'll run to the drugstore and get it. I'll be back in a few minutes. Thank you for saying I can stay." He rattled it all off as quickly as he could, then left before she could say anything else that would get him into trouble.

She heard the front door bang shut and went to the window. She watched him running up the street. What was she going to do with him until tomorrow? Then she remembered that she had to call Harry and cancel their date. Her grandson was already making her life difficult.

28

A Close Shave

What was he going to tell his grandmother when he showed up without his bag? It was always harder to come up with a story when he had to think about it too much. He was at the drugstore soda fountain eating a dish of vanilla ice cream with hot-fudge sauce working on something he could sell. The hot fudge was collected around the ice cream like a moat around a castle. Hot and cold didn't get on much better than oil and water until you brought them together in your mouth. Then it was a different story. He dipped the tip of his spoon into the hot fudge, shaved off a curl of ice cream, and brought them home. Small bites. Make it last. He needed time.

I can't say I lost it, he thought. I can't say I left it on the bus. Too late for that. Maybe the lady at the cash register stole it. No good. Alice probably knew the lady and she'd call and find out that there never was a bag and that would be the end of that. And him. Maybe somebody robbed the drugstore and took his bag thinking there was something valuable in it. Too complicated. And, anyway, Alice would find out quick enough that the drugstore hadn't been robbed at all. He had to remember that he was in a small town. People knew each other. News traveled fast. For a brief moment he considered telling her the truth, but, given their encounter, he had no faith in that idea. None at all. Clearly she had no interest in his welfare. She'd call his mother, and he'd be worse off than he was at the moment.

Maybe his bag was stolen when nobody was looking and there wasn't the slightest clue who took it. That might work. Chances were Alice wouldn't call the drugstore about that. And if she found out about it tomorrow, so what? He'd be gone. He decided to start with that story and see where it took him.

Alice had Harry on the telephone. Her problem was calling off their date without telling him the reason. She wasn't ready to think of herself as a grandmother. For one thing, she didn't think she was nearly old enough. She certainly didn't look it. She felt far younger than sixty. And if she wasn't ready, then it wasn't anybody else's business. Besides, Harry was ten years younger than she was, and she didn't want to do anything to rock that boat. Not when it was sailing so smoothly. She wanted things to go on the way they were. She had no expectations beyond that. She'd be too old for him in a few years. It would end then. Nature would make sure of it. In the meantime, she was having fun. He was good company. Smart. Funny. Excellent in the romance department.

"Why don't we just have dinner?" Harry said. "I haven't seen you in a week."

"You're the one who went away," Alice said.

"Business is business. You could have come with me."

"I'm no good at that sort of thing."

"Going away with me?"

"Trying to fill my day in a strange place while you're at meetings."

"I missed you."

How was she supposed to respond to that? He'd never said it before. An unwritten rule broken. Had she missed him? She had. She simply didn't want to admit it to herself.

"Tomorrow night," she said. "We'll have dinner then."

"I hope whatever you have goes away by then," Harry said.

"Oh, it will be gone," she said. "I can guarantee that."

The doorbell rang. A high note followed by a low. "Come at seven," she said.

It was Sidney at the door, looking dejected, appropriately put out by the theft of his bag. He told her the story on the way to the sitting room, which was just off the studio. Three of its walls were papered with faded flowers. The fourth was a bay window filled with violets. Her chair and a plain rectangular writing table were set in front of it, giving her a view of the street. Two smaller chairs, two glass-doored bookcases crammed with books, and a small television set completed the room.

"I'll call the police," she said. She was outraged. "People don't get robbed in Middleport."

"There was a policeman there," Sidney said hurriedly. "He was buying gum. I told him what happened and he wrote it all down. He said there wasn't much chance of finding it. I told him I was staying with you. He knew who you were."

"Well, I'm calling the drugstore and yelling at somebody," she said, heading for the telephone.

"Please don't," he pleaded, following her.

"They're responsible."

"I'm responsible. The lady at the cash register felt terrible. I don't want her to get in trouble. She didn't do anything wrong. I shouldn't have left it there."

She looked at him, phone in hand, considering his request. She liked his sense of fairness.

"I bought a toothbrush," he said, taking it from his pocket. It was red. "I can buy some new clothes in the morning. I don't need much. I'll go before the bus leaves. I saw a store up there that sells clothes." He looked at her hopefully. He'd given it his best shot.

She looked through her things and came up with a Quahog Festival T-shirt and an old bathing suit of Harry's, which required a belt made of package twine snugged tightly around Sidney's waist to keep it up. Alice was just barely able to keep herself from laughing when he presented himself in the kitchen. His skinny legs poked out from the baggy trunks, which ended well below his knees. The sleeves of the T-shirt hung down below his elbows. She put his clothes in the washing machine, one of those washer-on-the-bottom, dryer-on-the-top deals, then pressed on with the matter of dinner.

"What do you mean you don't eat meat?" she asked, her tone openly hostile.

"I don't like it and I don't eat it," he said, looking her right in the eye, his arms crossed over his chest.

"How do you know what you like and don't like? You're not old enough. You haven't experienced anything. You haven't been anywhere."

"I don't eat meat, that's all. If you want to kill me, go ahead. But I'm not eating meat. Never again."

"Why?"

"What difference does it make?"

"I want to know what would possess you to give up meat. You're still growing. You need the protein. I can't believe your mother lets you get away with it."

"I don't eat meat because it comes from animals. Animals have babies. I won't eat anything that has children."

"Not even a chicken?"

"No."

"Chickens are stupid."

"So are a lot of people."

"Eggs?"

"No."

"Not even eggs?"

"There might be an embryo in one of them."

"Fish?"

"No."

"Shrimp?"

"No shrimp."

"What do you eat?"

"Spaghetti. Cheese. Cereal." He had to think of something else fast. "Rice and beans." That was a good one.

"You can't live on that."

"Vegetables," he said, even though he wasn't overly fond of them. Well, he did like potatoes and carrots and peas and, oddly enough, broccoli. "Fruit."

"I have beans," she said.

"That's fine."

"You can open the can and heat them," she said. "You'll have them on toast." She expected him to protest that it wasn't enough food, or that he didn't eat toast, or some such, but he just nodded.

"I can make toast," he said. "I can do lots of things."

When they sat down to eat she eyed his plate. The toast was burned. With the beans poured on top it looked like something the cat threw up. "Beans on toast is very popular in England," she said when she saw his expression. She sat across from him with her leftover flank steak and slices of beefsteak tomato. "You sure you don't want any tomato?" she asked a second time.

"I'm sure," he said.

"You said you liked vegetables."

"Tomatoes aren't vegetables, they're fruit."

"You said you liked fruit."

"I don't like tomatoes."

"What do you put on your spaghetti?"

"That's sauce. It's different."

She concluded that there was no sense to be made of this and started eating her dinner. "I'll tell you where I draw the line with food," she said. "I draw the line with cats and dogs. I won't eat cats and dogs. I don't care how they're cooked. I don't care what you put on them."

Sidney laughed.

She looked at him with surprise and saw his face transformed in a spasm of happiness. He was a delightful-looking kid when he laughed. It lasted slightly longer than a nanosecond.

"Do you have ketchup?" he asked. "I like ketchup on my beans, even if it's made from tomatoes."

"In the door of the refrigerator. Help yourself."

Sidney left the table and returned with a plastic bottle of ketchup, which he had to thump, pump, squeeze, and shake in order to get enough of the red ooze onto his beans to satisfy him.

"What's your father up to these days?" she asked after they'd settled into eating.

"He sells rugs."

"You mean those bad hairpieces?"

"I mean what you put on a floor."

"Carpets."

"Carpets, rugs, what's the difference?"

"I never knew a man who had so many jobs," she said. "Is he still good-looking? Well, you wouldn't see him that way. Is he married?"

Sidney shook his head. His mouth was full of beans.

"I'm not surprised. Sid thinks he's Peter Pan. His idea of a long time from now is tomorrow."

"Stop picking on him," Sidney said. He was upset. He didn't like it when someone spoke poorly of his father. Whatever else he felt about Sid, he recognized inside himself that he loved him.

She gave Sidney a long look. It occurred to her that he must lead something less than an idyllic life. "You still going back and forth between them?"

He nodded. His mouth was full again. He was pumping it in. Feeding fuel to the furnace. And anyway, he didn't want to talk about his parents.

"At least your father has charm. That jerk your mother married doesn't know the meaning of the word. I told her not to be in such a hurry the second time. I told her to give herself a breather. See if she couldn't come up with something better. She told me to take a hike. At least she stood up to me. That's progress."

"Why don't you like my mother?"

"Why doesn't your mother like me?"

"I don't know," he said, "maybe she does. Maybe she just doesn't want to say so."

"I don't dislike your mother. We just don't get along."

"Do you love her?"

The question startled Alice, not because she didn't

know the answer but because she hadn't thought about it in such a long time.

"I was wondering how people felt about their children when their children grew up," he continued. "Do your parents leave you alone then, or do they keep telling you what to do?"

"I never told her what to do," Alice said. But of course that wasn't true. She'd told Meredith what to do all the time when she was growing up. She'd kept telling her what to do even after she ran off. Or she'd tried to. Meredith didn't have enough backbone to take care of herself. She was too fearful of life. Alice had tried to tell her what to do the last time they'd spoken on the telephone. That was two years ago. Almost three.

Sidney tried to picture his mother as a child, living here with his grandmother. He'd seen photographs of her when she was his age. Her expression always seemed to have an air of expectation about it, as though she were living in the next moment rather than the one she was in. Even when she smiled she seemed perplexed.

"They can't keep shipping you back and forth between them forever," she said. "You should stay in one place for high school at least. Otherwise you'll never have any friends."

"I don't need friends," he said, sweeping the last of

the beans onto his fork with his final crust of toast. "I don't have time for friends." He stuffed the whole thing into his mouth.

She watched him drain his glass of milk. He was in desperate straits, this boy with a man's seriousness. It seemed to her that he was holding on to the sheer wall of a rock face with his fingertips. It made her angry. She'd call his mother in the morning.

29

Alice's Solution

It was seven in the morning and Alice couldn't wait any longer. She didn't care that there was a three-hour time difference between Middleport and Seattle. Meredith could get up in the dark to talk about her son. She checked Sidney, who was sleeping the sleep of angels in the bed she'd set up on the back porch. He seemed, for the moment at least, to be at peace with himself and the world.

She made her coffee and went to the sitting room and collected her thoughts. Clearly one of Sidney's parents should take him full-time. He could spend summers with the other one. The case could be made that he should be with his mother and see his father on holidays. At least he'd have some sort of family life that way. Even if Devers was a hard case. But summers and holidays away from his classmates at critical times would mean he'd miss out on a social life. He needed to be with his friends when they were on vacation from school. She knew Meredith would jump at this idea. She'd talk to Sid. She suspected that it might be a great relief to him to have his son well looked after on a permanent basis. He could travel to Seattle when he wanted to see Sidney. Sidney might even go to Los Angeles for occasional visits if he wanted to. Alice would broker this arrangement, say goodbye to Sidney, and get on with the plans that she'd made for herself.

Meredith's sleepy voice answered on the third ring with a panicked "Hello?" Alice could hear Devers complaining in the background.

"It's Alice," Alice said.

"Who?" In her fog, Meredith couldn't place the name.

"Your mother."

There was a roar of silence at the other end. What did her mother want at four in the morning? Was she drunk? Maybe she was sick.

"You don't want to talk to me," Alice said, "that's fine. But you're going to listen. I've been talking to

Sidney and I've concluded that something has to be done about how he's being brought up."

"What?" Meredith found her voice.

"Your son. Sidney. I've been talking to him. You remember your son."

"Why would you talk to Sidney? I don't recall your ever showing the slightest interest. Is there something wrong? Why are you calling me?"

"Tell her to call back later." It was Devers. "Tell her Sidney is none of her business."

"Of course there's something wrong," Alice said. "This shipping him back and forth has got to stop. It's not healthy. He has enough liabilities. He has no friends. He'll end up a recluse."

"Did Sid put you up to this?"

"You have to get permanent custody, Meredith. Sid can visit. Your son needs stability. He lacks confidence."

"Couldn't we please talk about this later?"

"He'll be awake later. I don't want him to know that I spoke to you. He'll think I'm reporting on him."

Meredith sat bolt upright in bed. "What do you mean he'll be awake later? Where are you?"

"I'm home and Sidney is sleeping on the porch. I'll talk to Sid. I'm sure I can convince him that it's in Sidney's best interest—"

"Sidney's with you?" Meredith's hysteria built by the word. "He can't be with you. He's in Los Angeles with Sid. What's he doing there? How did he get there?"

"He came by bus. What's the matter with you? Isn't he on his way to Harvard for a week of summer school? That's what he told me."

"I'm going to straighten that boy out." Devers again. "We're going to come to an understanding."

"I'm coming to get him!" Meredith shrieked. "I'll be there tonight. As soon as I can. I'm going to the airport right now."

"Wait!" Alice yelled, but it was already too late. The phone was dead in her hand. She hit the redial.

"It's too early in the morning to be calling people," Devers said angrily, after picking up the receiver on the first ring.

"Put my daughter back on," Alice demanded.

"She's in the bathroom crying," Devers said. "Whatever you have to say to her you can say to me."

"Sidney came all the way across the country by himself on the bus and this is the first you're hearing of it? What kind of parents are you?"

"Ship the kid back," Devers said. "I'm not letting his mother spend all that money just to do it in person. It's too expensive."

"I don't think so," Alice said.

"I'm telling you to put him on a plane. I'll send you a check."

"Don't tell me what to do. If you want Sidney, you'll have to come get him." It was Alice's turn to hang up. She was seething. She called information. There was only one Sidney T. Mellon, Senior, listed in Los Angeles.

"Your son has run away," she said when Sid finally picked up the phone. "This is your former mother-in-law. He's here with me."

"Alice?" Sid was a slow riser. Not a morning person.

"Apparently he left you and came across the country on a bus."

"He's supposed to be in Seattle."

"Meredith is coming to get him and so are you."

"If Meredith is coming, I don't see why I have to—"

She cut him off. "He had two parents when he was born," she said, her voice as hard as the business end of a hammer, "and he has two now, even if you are divorced."

"I can't take the time off."

"I didn't call to have a conversation with you, Sid. You're his father. Get on the first plane that has room for you and get back here. Your son needs your time and attention."

She hung up, satisfied that they'd both come. Now she had to deal with Sidney. She resisted the urge to wake him and vent her anger. She'd deal with him later.

She took her coffee into the studio. Sidney was right about the painting. It was all surface. It stunk. They all stunk. She was sixty years old. What had she done with her life? What would she do with what was left of it?

30

Once More into the Breach

Dressed, rested, feeling less pain than he had the day before, Sidney contemplated the day ahead. He and Alice were having a silent breakfast of toast and orange marmalade, both of them lost momentarily in their own thoughts. For Sidney it was a matter of how quickly he could escape his grandmother's clutches. He wanted to be on the first bus to Boston. After that, he had no idea what was in store for him.

Alice contemplated the day ahead as well. She saw nothing but trouble once he knew she was onto him, but there was no other way to keep him from leaving. She couldn't think of a story that would keep him here. That left the truth. She'd find some way to keep him occupied. She'd make it clear that he wasn't to leave her sight. He was a handful, and once he knew that his parents were coming, he'd be worse.

"I spoke to your mother this morning," she said finally. She watched him carefully, trying to read his reaction.

Sidney felt like somebody had punched him in the stomach, like he'd gotten all the wind knocked out of him. He felt betrayed. He shook his head from side to side as though by denying what he'd just heard he could make it go away.

"I also spoke to your father."

He stood up, holding on to the table for support. He felt light-headed. He wasn't ready for it to be over. He hadn't arrived at his destination.

"Sit down," she said firmly. "There isn't going to be any monkey business."

He sat. It was his own stupid fault for coming here. He should have known better than to trust his grandmother.

"You lied to me, Sidney. I don't like people who lie to me. It's a bad habit and it will get you into a lot of trouble."

"I suppose you always tell the truth," he said.

"Not always," she said. "I'm not proud of that. You're a kid. You ran away. You could have gotten yourself in a lot of trouble."

"What difference does it make what I do? You

184

didn't like me before and you don't like me now. You told on me. You turned me in."

"You show up here out of nowhere and think I'm not going to say something to your parents? You're too young to be on your own. You'll end up on the streets or worse."

"So what? What do you care?"

"You say that a lot."

"What do you care?" he repeated. He was already thinking about how he could escape.

"They're on their way here, Sidney," she said. "Your mother and father."

"I don't feel well," he said, getting to his feet, his hands on his stomach. "I have to go to the bathroom." He started for it, hoping to occupy her with concern. "I always have to go when I get upset."

"They'll get in sometime tonight and be here in the morning and you'll be here when they arrive. Meanwhile, you and I are going to spend the day together." She lifted her coffee cup and sipped at its contents, eyeing him over the rim. Her expression warned him not to try anything.

Sidney took a step toward the bathroom, then cut hard to the left, then to the right, and ran through the sitting room to the studio. It took several moments for Alice to move. By the time she'd realized what was happening and put down her cup and pushed herself away from the table, he was in the front hall. By the time she got herself up to speed, he was out the front door and onto the street. She ran after him, stopping after half a block because she was winded. He was, in any event, far too fast for her. She made her way back to the apartment as quickly as she could to get her car keys.

He ran across a yard, ducking under a clothesline filled with sheets and underwear and into a lane, then jumped a stone wall near its bend and found himself in a thicket of dense brush and trees. He thrashed through this until he came to another stone wall. On the other side of it was an area, perhaps five acres in all, of near wilderness. There was a birch-topped hill and tall grass that swayed in the morning breeze and berry bushes and poison ivy and a small pond, which was filled with cattails and not much water. There were bees and yellow jackets and dragonflies, and the sound of rustling grasses and stirring branches. There wasn't a building or another person to be seen.

Sidney marveled at this secret Eden. He could hide here. At least until dark. Then he could get to the main road and hitchhike to Boston. But they'd all be looking for him by then. His grandmother would surely have gone to the police. At least he could stay here for a while. He could gather his wits and decide what to do later.

He made his way to the top of the hill. From there he looked down at the pond and the scattering of houses beyond it that swept out toward the bay. A dog barked in the distance and was answered by another. On the leeward side of the hill he found a small clearing among some slender birches and sat. It was peaceful here. There were songbirds to reassure him. It felt secure. He put his face to the sun and closed his eyes.

He heard a plane overhead, a passenger jet on its way to the Providence airport. He opened his eyes and craned his neck to see it. In a few hours his parents would be here. He felt a flood of tears rising inside him and pushed them back down. He wasn't done. He'd do what he had to. Nobody would stop him. He got to his feet, determined to finish what he'd started, then saw them coming.

There were two boys, one considerably larger than the other, and a tall, slim girl with short raven hair. He thought about trying to run, then decided that he didn't want to. He was tired of not standing up for himself. He decided to act tough. It was a matter of attitude.

"How ya doing?" Sidney said, flipping the words out, pushing on without waiting for a response. "I got lost back here and I'm looking for the way into town. I'm catching the bus to Boston. I'm going to play football for Boston College. I kick field goals."

"Town's over that way," the girl said. She pointed. His eyes were riveted to her face, to her eyes, which were emerald green. Her voice was small and sweet and magical in its quietness. "Just keep going until you come out on West Carpenter Street. You're going to play football?"

"I was a soccer player in Brazil," he said. "A lot of soccer players become football kickers." He couldn't stop looking at her. She was taller than he was but about the same age, with luminous features, especially when she smiled, which she was doing now.

"He don't look like no football player to me," the large boy said. "He looks more like a pizza." He was nearly six feet tall and gangly. The other boy was Sidney's size.

"More like a melon," the small one said. "Like a Melonhead."

Sidney snapped. It was once too often. His head down, his arms flailing punches, he rushed the small boy with a yell. "Don't call me Melonhead!"

The target of his charge stepped neatly aside, took hold of Sidney's arm, and pulled him forward. Sidney's momentum suddenly doubled, and he went flying by the boy, fell hard to the ground, and grunted loudly.

"They were just kidding," the girl said.

"Yeah," the large boy said, "can't you take a joke?"

"No," Sidney shouted, getting to his feet. "My head's not a joke." He charged again and found himself flying through the air again and hit the ground again, only this time harder. His grunt was louder. It hurt. It took him longer to get up. The third time Sidney feigned the charge, changed directions, and got his arms around the boy, who promptly slipped the hold and threw Sidney over his shoulder. His fourth charge was his last. He landed a glancing blow to his adversary's head, then felt himself turning, twisting, and hitting the ground on his back in what seemed a single motion. He stayed put.

"You don't give up easy," the small boy said. "I don't want to hurt you."

"Yeah," the large boy said. "We don't like to hurt anybody."

"I'm George," the small boy said. He was smiling a little now. "This is my brother, Ben. We're fraternal twins."

Sidney just stared at them. He didn't know what to say.

"I'm Isabella," the girl said. "Who are you?"

"Joe Mechanic," Sidney said. "In Brazil they called me José."

"We'll see you around, Joe," George said. He started off down the hill, Ben behind him.

"Yeah," Ben said, "we'll see you around."

"I'll catch up," Isabella said, then turned her attention to Sidney, who was astonished to find himself alone with her.

"Are you all right?" she asked him with genuine

concern. He could hear it in her voice. He mattered.

He nodded, even though he hurt everywhere. All the soreness from his beating in New York was back. His face was dirty. His pants were torn.

"George didn't want to hurt you," she said. "He could have. He knows martial arts." She touched his face where it was bruised. "It took a lot of guts to keep going after him like that. He was impressed. I could tell. I know I was. I'm named after Queen Isabella of Spain. My last name's Spring." She held out her hand.

He shook it. His palm was sweaty. The radiance of her proximity was almost more than he could bear. He could only glance at her from this short distance. His tongue felt like a lead weight.

"Don't worry about your head," she said. "I think you're cute."

Sidney couldn't believe what he was hearing. Somebody thought Melonhead was cute? Somebody as beautiful and charming and wonderful as Isabella? He felt his face flushing, and he hated it. He hated how he looked. She was just being kind to him. Like you would to a stray dog you happened on.

"I mean it," she said, then left.

He watched her go, then wondered if she'd ever been there at all. He put his hand to his face where she'd touched him. He felt a pull at his heart.

31

Waiting for the Ax to Fall

Sidney gathered his forces, made his way down the hill, and found the path that led to the village. The traffic sign for Route 1 pointed him in the right direction for Boston. This was his last chance. Somebody would take pity on him. Somebody would give him a ride if he stuck out his thumb. Somebody did. Alice. He was in the car before he realized who it was.

"Do you have any idea how much trouble you are?" she yelled at him as she hit the button to lock the doors and stepped on the gas.

"If I'd known it was you I wouldn't have gotten in," he yelled back.

She made a U-turn and headed for her apartment. "I've been driving around this village looking for you for an hour," she said. "I was . . . Never mind what I was. I'm not letting you out of my sight until your parents show up. Then they're welcome to you."

The rest of the day was mostly a blur to Sidney. He lived it in a state of hyperanxiety. His parents were coming. They were somewhere over the country, flying at thirty-five thousand feet at six hundred miles an hour toward him. What if Devers was coming, too? He prayed that his stepfather would stay in Seattle. He'd give anything for that. He was in plenty of trouble already. If Devers came, something terrible would happen.

After he cleaned up, Alice took him to buy another set of clothes, new shoes, and two pairs of socks and underwear. She gave him no choice in the selection. He didn't protest.

"I don't want them to see you in poor condition," she said. "You'll be bright-eyed and bushy-tailed when they get here."

After that they went to the diner for lunch. Sidney ordered a cheese sandwich.

"What kind of cheese?" the counterman asked.

"What kind of cheese do you have?" Sidney inquired.

"Swiss, American, and Muenster."

"Swiss has holes in it," Sidney said.

"That's right. It does. It has holes."

"What's the difference between American and Muenster?" Sidney asked.

The counterman gave Alice a look.

"He'll have American," Alice said.

"On white toast with mustard," Sidney added quickly.

"I don't want them to say I didn't feed you," Alice said. "He'll have French fries with it."

"I don't like French fries," Sidney said. "They cook them in fat. They're greasy. I'll have pie instead."

"It has to be apple pie or berry pie," she said. "Something with fruit in it. It has to have some nutritional value."

Sidney looked at the counterman.

"Blueberry, strawberry, peach, apple, and rhubarb," the counterman said, his expression hopeful that this business would be concluded quickly.

"I like them all except rhubarb," Sidney said. "And blueberry." Since Lilly and Hiram, he'd lost his taste for blueberries. He thought about it. "Peach," he said finally. "I'll have peach. With ice cream on it."

"What kind of ice cream?" the counterman asked.

"What kind do you have?" Sidney asked.

The counterman rolled his eyes. "We have fourteen flavors," he said.

"What are they?"

"Vanilla, chocolate, strawberry, coffee, black raspberry, chocolate chip, chocolate nut brownie, maple walnut, butter pecan, mint chip, chocolate swirl, peach, pistachio, and coconut."

"Oh, that's easy," Sidney said. "I'll have vanilla."

Alice stifled her laugh. "There's nothing wrong with your appetite," she said, after she'd ordered a bowl of clam chowder.

Sidney was hungry enough to eat a horse, figuratively speaking. If this was going to be one of his last meals as a free man, he wanted to get as much into him that he liked as he possibly could. When the counterman sped by with an armload of orders, he politely ordered a root beer.

"What do you think of Middleport?" Alice asked to make conversation.

"I wish I'd never seen it," Sidney said.

So much for small talk.

After lunch, Alice decided to show Sidney the state university. She figured a half hour to get there, an hour to walk around, and a half hour to get back. Two hours closer to getting rid of him. And if he saw something to look forward to, it might improve his disposition, though she doubted it. Besides which, she couldn't think of anything else to do.

They parked at the edge of the campus and walked past the fraternity houses and through the stone gates. Summer session was over, and only the odd maintenance man and occasional professor were to be seen. The empty buildings seemed like huge ghost ships adrift in a sea of close-cropped lawn. Alice hadn't been to the campus in a long time. She didn't like it as much as she used to. She'd gone to school here in the late fifties and early sixties, when grand open spaces lived in harmony with classic stone and brick structures.

Sidney looked about with momentary interest. He'd thought vaguely about going to college someday because he understood it as a way to get free from home. But that would be six years from now, and he couldn't wait that long. He thought about running again. It would take her a good fifteen minutes to get back to her car, and by then he might be able to get a ride.

"Why'd you run away?" she asked, as though reading his mind.

He acted like he hadn't heard the question.

"Are things that bad?"

He looked around and eyed the man who was cutting the grass, riding his lawn mower as though it was some kind of huge farm machine. Two streets up he saw a campus police car drift by, as lazy as the August afternoon itself.

"What's bothering you in one place is just as likely to bother you in the next," she said. "Your problems follow you." She thought she sounded like a character from a bad movie. Cheap advice was worth what you paid for it. Why was she getting involved, anyway? He wasn't her problem.

"Are things so bad that you can't stay with either one of them?" she asked, despite her advice to herself. When he didn't answer, she tried again. "Where were you going?"

He ignored her. He was defeated, but only temporarily. He'd find a way.

She began to wonder if he'd come all this distance to get her help. Even if he couldn't articulate it, maybe he needed her to make peace in his family.

"I want to know what's going on in that mind of yours," she said. "What did you think you were up to?"

"I was going to Boston," he said, "then I was going to turn around and go right back. It was just a trip. Something I could talk about when my teacher asked me what I did this summer. They always ask you what you did. I thought it would be a good experience."

"Horse potatoes."

"Horse potatoes?"

"What the stable hands clean up." She smiled. "You tell a good story. I'll give you that."

"If I hadn't been robbed in New York City, I never would have gotten off here," he said.

"You were robbed?"

"Forget it."

"Is that how you got all those bruises?"

"I fell down the stairs."

"Do you know how to tell the truth about anything?"

"Yes," he said. "I don't like this place. That's the truth. If you let me get away, I promise you'll never see me again. That will make us both happy."

When she didn't protest, she saw a spasm of hurt shoot across his face, then disappear beneath a protective coating of indifference.

He looked up at the sun, which was midafternoon high. He was running out of time.

On the way back to Alice's apartment, they stopped at Sawyer's Market to buy dinner. Sidney studied the live lobsters in the big glass tank. He whispered to them that if it was within his power he'd set them all free. He'd buy them and let them loose in the harbor. He'd set all the captive animals in the world free if he could, then find them safe places to live. After the lobsters would come the live fish, then all the chickens and beef cattle, then all the lions and monkeys and bears and elephants and everything else. Every living creature that people ate or killed or imprisoned.

"I could pick out some cookies and ice cream," he said to Alice as she decided which piece of scrod to buy.

"We'll pick them out together," she said. "I'm not letting you out of my sight. None of your tricks."

Scrod for her, spaghetti for him. Oreo cookies and chocolate and vanilla ice cream for both of them.

The rest of the afternoon passed too slowly for her and too quickly for him. He needed an opening, just a small one, and he'd be gone. She called Harry to cancel their evening, and they argued for the first time in their relationship. She hung up, unhappy with him and even unhappier with herself. Sidney looked at a magazine but didn't see a word of it. Alice did the crossword puzzle. She retreated to her studio. There was no way out of the apartment except to pass her in that room, so eventually he wandered in. He tried to sidle casually to the door, a slow inch at a time. He needed that little edge. She watched his every move.

"Come here and tell me what you think of it now," she said, stepping back from the easel and eyeing him. "I've been working on it."

"What do you care what I think about anything?" he said, frustrated again in his attempt to break free.

"Just tell me what you think. You must have an opinion. You must know whether you like something or not."

Reluctantly, he moved into position to see the painting. He looked at it for a long moment, then looked at her. "I don't like it," he said.

"Don't hold anything back," she said.

"I don't like it a lot," he said.

"What do you mean, you don't like it?" she asked defensively. "What kind of constructive comment is that?"

"Okay," he said, "I really don't like it. How's that?"

"Why? Because it's not a nice pretty picture of a house or a field of flowers?"

"Because it gives me a headache," he said. He wasn't going to let her push him around.

"You don't know anything about art."

He started for the sitting room. He'd had enough.

"What kind of education are you getting out there in the Wild West anyway?"

"No education. I hate school."

"What kind of attitude is that?"

"I don't like people talking at me all day long, telling me what to think and how to behave. I like to do things. I like to read. I like to think. I don't like to take tests." He was getting angry.

"Where do you think you'll get in life without an education?"

"Who said I want to get anywhere?"

"What's your mother have to say about this?"

"Nothing."

"You're twelve years old and already you're throwing your life away."

"It's my life. I can do what I want with it. Besides,

I don't see anybody doing so great with theirs. My mother is married to that loser Devers and is afraid to stand up to him. And my father sells rugs and chases women."

"That's enough, Sidney."

"You don't care about anybody but yourself."

"You know what?" Alice yelled at him, "let's spend the rest of the day out of each other's way."

"That's okay with me," Sidney yelled back. "I'd rather be alone than be with you."

"The feeling is mutual."

"I never want to see you again."

"It's a deal."

He returned to the porch and the magazine. She resumed her painting. They passed the next hour and a half in silence. Dinner required her to give directions, and they agreed to talk again but only about that.

He put on the pot of water, then emptied the jar of sauce into a pan to heat. When the water boiled, he dropped in half the box of spaghetti. Alice cooked her fish. She helped him pour the spaghetti into the strainer. She had to get a bowl down from the shelf because he wasn't tall enough to reach it. He thanked her. They agreed not to talk during dinner.

"I'm sorry," he said when they rose to clear the table. "I don't like it when I get mad."

"Accepted," she said. "I don't like it when I get

mad either." She started for the sink, then stopped and looked back. Sidney stood there, dishes in hand, not moving. "What is it now?"

"You didn't say you were sorry too."

"I'm not the one—" she started to say, then changed her mind. "Okay. I'm sorry too."

Sidney nodded and moved past her to the sink. She followed, wondering how far down you'd have to dig before you discovered who he really was.

They washed and dried the dishes without conversation. They watched television for a while. She made herself a cup of tea. He prepared two dishes of ice cream, which he served with cookies stuck in the tops of the scoops so they looked like eyes.

The first call came at nine-thirty. It was from Meredith. She and Devers had arrived at the Providence airport. "We just this minute got in," she said, breathless from hurrying to the pay phone. "We have to rent a car. We'll be there in forty-five minutes."

"Not tonight," Alice said, with a measured calm she didn't feel. "Sid's not here yet, and there's no meeting until he shows up." Her eyes shifted to Sidney, who was up out of his chair and standing stiffly, like he'd received an electric shock.

"What do you mean, not tonight?" Meredith shouted. "I don't care about Sid. Do you have any idea what kind of day I've had getting across the country?"

201

"It's late," Alice said, "and I'm tired and you're tired and we all need a good night's rest."

"I want my son. Put him on the phone."

Alice held the receiver out to Sidney, who shook his head violently. She put her hand over the mouthpiece. "Better do it now and break the ice," she said. "It'll make it easier tomorrow."

Sidney swallowed hard and took the phone from his grandmother. He looked at it for a moment, like it was a poisonous snake, then spoke into it. "Hello," he said. He could barely get the word out.

"Are you all right?" his mother asked, barely able to control herself. "Why did you do it? How could you do this to me?"

"I'm fine," Sidney said, responding to the first question and letting the others pass.

"We have some talking to do, Sidney."

"Let me have the phone." Sidney heard Devers's voice in the background. He handed the phone to Alice. He was vibrating like a hummingbird. All the color had drained from his face.

"I'm coming to get you right now," Meredith said, keeping the phone from her husband, thinking that Sidney was still on. "I don't care what she says."

"Not tonight," Alice said, her voice firm in the way Meredith remembered it when there was to be no compromise. "The doors are locked and the lights are about to go off. Your son is in perfectly good working order. You'll come for breakfast at eight and we'll sort everything out then. I'll have coffee. You bring the doughnuts." She hung up.

Sidney's heart raced. His breathing was labored. Devers was here. He couldn't stand it.

"Take a deep breath," Alice said. "Let it out slowly."

"I can't," Sidney gasped, trying to keep himself from hyperventilating.

"You can if you try. Watch me." She took in a long, slow breath of air through her nose, then let it out slowly through her mouth. It sounded like a lovely, deep sigh. "In through your nose, out through your mouth. Feel yourself breathing, Sidney. Hear yourself breathing. Don't think about anything. Follow my rhythm." Her tone was gentle, persuasive.

Sidney's breathing began to slow down. He focused on the air going in and out. It went lower and lower into his body. He began to hear the internal hum of it.

"Drop your shoulders," she said. "Just let them plop down. Let all the tension in your body float away."

An hour later the telephone rang again. Sidney froze. Alice answered it.

"I just arrived in Boston," Sid said.

"Boston will never be the same," Alice said.

"Can we get through this without the wisecracks, Alice?"

"I don't know, Sid, can we? Can you pay attention to your son? Can you do what's right? Eight o'clock tomorrow morning. My place. Be on time."

"Don't hang up," Sid yelled.

"We'll talk then," Alice said. She started to replace the receiver.

"I want to know how he's doing."

"For a kid who doesn't want anything to do with anybody, he's doing great." She hung up and had to talk Sidney down from the window ledge of anxiety for the second time that night.

"I know it isn't easy," she said, "but you're old enough to have a say in all this. Do you have a preference? Would you rather live with one of them than the other?"

Sidney flashed on the judge's office. He was six years old again and no more capable of answering the question now than he was then. All he could do was stare helplessly at his grandmother.

"Think about it tonight," she said. "Let me know in the morning. You can't keep going back and forth between them. You have to pick somebody to live with. It has to be settled."

In bed, Alice replayed her day with Sidney. He needed so much. He had so little. Sidney led her to Meredith. Her daughter had to be strong for Sidney. He had to know that when he fell, she'd be there to

catch him. With her eyes closed and her hands rest-
ing on her chest, she drifted off to sleep with images
of her daughter as a young child in her mind, her
happy, carefree child.

Sidney fell quickly into the deep sleep that comes
from exhaustion. It was as though the weight of the
day ahead was so heavy that it crushed him into the
darkness of a bottomless pit.

32

Sidney's Choice

When they arrived—first his mother and Devers, who were early, then Sid, who was late—Sidney was gone. Alice had wanted him to sleep as late as he could. He'd need all the strength he could muster. She didn't go to wake him until seven-fifteen. He'd made the bed, left his old clothes folded neatly on top of the pillow, and gone out the window. Why hadn't she remembered the window? Why hadn't she checked on him during the night? She'd called the police station and spoken with Sandra, who was Sergeant Whitmore, who'd said that they'd keep a lookout for the small boy with the large, round head. All this Alice explained to Meredith, who was hysterical. Then Devers took her off in their rental car, and Sid and Alice drove off in hers to join the search.

Sidney had been up since shortly after midnight. He'd come to consciousness with the same suddenness that had taken him off to sleep, and he knew with absolute certainty the moment his eyes sprang open what he had to do. He wasn't ready to face his parents. He didn't want to see Devers and hear that voice. His journey wasn't finished. He'd crossed the line into the next town in the thick darkness of early morning. He had what was left of his fifty dollars and an urgency in his step. He'd stayed well off the road when he could, and there hadn't been much traffic, which was a blessing.

At sun's first light, when he was far enough away from his grandmother's house, he'd stuck his thumb into the air and gotten his first ride. From a young couple in a tomato-red pickup truck. He'd told them that his name was Hector Nordstrom, no relation to the family who owned the department store, that he lived on a farm, and that he had the day off to go see the Red Sox play baseball at Fenway Park. And he sure did appreciate being able to save on bus fare because that meant he could afford an extra hot dog at the ballpark. They took him all the way to Attleboro, Massachusetts, where they wished him well. An interesting boy, they said to each other as they drove off. An unusually pleasant disposition. They smiled at each other about the size and shape of the boy's head. They found something strangely reassuring in it.

Sidney's next ride took him to Plymouth. The driver was an old man who drove slowly and enjoyed the company of such a bright and entertaining young man. And so cheerful. Sidney was Busby Spackle on this leg of his journey. He said he was going to see Plymouth Rock, where the Pilgrims landed, because he was writing a paper on it for school. He figured that if he ever wrote all the papers he said he was writing, it would take him a year.

Alice called Sandra at the police station for the fifth time that morning. "Did you alert the Boston police?" she asked. "Did you hear anything?"

"Yes, I alerted the Boston police," Sandra said. "And no, we haven't heard anything. It could take time, Alice. I don't like saying it, but a million kids run away from home every year in this country. We don't find them all."

Alice kept this information to herself. "They're doing everything they can" was all she said to the others. She considered, for a moment, the idea of raising Sidney when he was found. If he was found. Please, God. She'd do a better job than she'd done with Meredith. She dismissed the thought. It was crazy.

"What we have to do is get Sidney more involved

with outside activities," Devers said. The voice of wisdom. "It's not healthy, all the time he spends alone. He needs to play sports and be more social. My son, William, can help him with that. William likes Sidney. They get along real well. I know I'm going to take more interest."

Meredith wanted to believe her husband when he sounded like this. She talked herself into it, even though she knew he'd disappoint her. If only she could leave him. If only it was possible. All she really wanted was her son back. She just wanted him to be all right and for the two of them to be together.

"What we have to do," Sid said, giving Devers a hard look, "is find out what Sidney wants. I'll do whatever it takes to make him happy. I don't want him to feel that he ever has to run away again."

Alice looked at Meredith. "Sidney has to be in one place or the other," she said, laying the issue out for her daughter to seize. "He can't keep going back and forth between you like a yo-yo. You have to come to some sort of arrangement."

Devers put his arm around Meredith and smiled at Alice. "I want him to be part of our family," he said. "He certainly doesn't have one in Los Angeles." He couldn't resist smirking at Sid. "He needs what a full-time family can give him."

"Whatever it takes," Sid said. He was feeling protective of his son, and it surprised him. A few days ago he couldn't wait to get rid of him. Now he wasn't so sure. He was definitely going to have to do something about Devers. The man was a menace. "Whatever Sidney decides is okay with me." He said it looking directly at Devers. He realized suddenly how much his son meant to him now that he was out of reach.

It took Sidney three rides and most of the rest of the day to reach his destination. He was Fargo Mackie, Carl Bang, and Winston Pullover. He never thought about the dangers of hitchhiking because he was in such a hurry and because they'd be looking for him on the bus. He was lucky to get rides with decent people and he knew it.

Outside Provincetown, at the far end of a beach, as far from people as he could get, he faced the open sea. Behind him was the continent he'd crossed, from one ocean to the other. He took off his shoes and socks and rolled up his pants and walked out into the Atlantic so he could feel it against his skin. He splashed water on his face, tasting the salt. He raised his fist to the sky and shook it in a rage.

"Why does it have to be like this?" he shouted as loudly as he could. "Why can't it be the way I want it?" There was only the wind and the breaking of waves upon the shore to answer him. He let loose a sob, a great wail that came from the depths of the

210

secret place inside him. He let it all out, everything he'd buried in there, until he was empty.

In the quiet that followed, Sidney thought about his journey. He wondered if Moses Longfellow had found his turquoise and if Gladys Winchester had made it to Los Angeles. He hoped so. He hoped that Shamus Flowers was living out his last days in Nashville happily. He hoped that Mona Lipp, with two *p*'s, was doing all right too. For a moment he could hear the music at the Starbright and he could hear her voice. He remembered that he owed her a postcard. His heart skipped a beat thinking about Isabella. Queen Isabella. He could still feel her touch on his face.

What were his choices? He could walk north toward Canada or he could start swimming for Europe or he could turn around and go back to face his life and make the best of it. Multiple choice with no fourth box that said, None of the above. Life would not always be this hard, he thought. It couldn't be.

The sun was setting when Sidney returned to the gas station he'd passed on the way to the beach. The evening light had taken on a warm, pinkish glow. He converted dollars to quarters and went outside to the pay phone, which was off by the air pump and water. He got the number from information, then placed the call. Alice answered on the first ring.

"I want to live with you," Sidney said. He could hear her breathing at the other end. "I want to live with you," he said again.

"Where are you?" Alice could barely control her voice.

"Is that Sidney?" Sidney could hear his mother yelling.

"I don't want to talk to anybody," Sidney said. "I want you to make them agree that I can live with you."

"I want to talk to my son," Meredith demanded. "Give me the phone."

"I thought you didn't like me," Alice said.

"I don't," Sidney said.

"Then why?"

Sidney could hear them all talking now, their voices raised, all of them wanting the phone.

"You asked me who I wanted to live with," Sidney responded. "I want to live with you. What difference does it make why?"

Alice told the others to be quiet so she could hear. "You're sure about this?" she asked Sidney.

"Promise me you'll make them agree," Sidney said.

"I promise I'll try," Alice said. "I'll do everything I can." What was she getting herself into? Why did he want her?

"I'll only live with you," he said. "If they don't agree, I'll run away again. Tell them that."

"I will," she said. "Where are you?"

"I'm in Provincetown," he said. "I'll take the bus back to Middleport. I can do that." He hung up before she could protest. He'd have this one last act of independence. At least for now.

On the way to catch the bus, Sidney contemplated living with his grandmother. Maybe it would work out. Who knew? Anyway, he saw it as his best chance. As for his head, so be it. If he had to be Melonhead, he'd be Melonhead. Everybody has something.